THE AMERICAN FUN-DEE

D. PATRICK CARROLL

America Star Books

© 2014 by D. Patrick Carroll.
All rights reserved. No part of this book may be reproduced, stored in a retrieval system or transmitted in any form or by any means without the prior written permission of the publishers, except by a reviewer who may quote brief passages in a review to be printed in a newspaper, magazine or journal.

First printing

All characters in this book are fictitious, and any resemblance to real persons, living or dead, is coincidental.

America Star Books has allowed this work to remain exactly as the author intended, verbatim, without editorial input.

Cover designed by Chad Carroll; Photograph by Chad Carroll.

Softcover 9781633825826
PUBLISHED BY AMERICA STAR BOOKS, LLLP
www.americastarbooks.com

Other America Star Books/Publish America published Novels by D. Patrick Carroll:

*Diabolical**
*El Diablo y Los Santos**
The Foundation Decision (The Final Chapter of the Diabolical Trilogy)*
*Degenerate**

*EBooks available for purchase on Amazon Kindle

This book is dedicated to my son who has designed the covers of my last two books, Chad G. Carroll, his lovely wife Melissa, my three beautiful granddaughters, Kristin and Samantha and the latest addition to their family, baby Milla.

FOREWORD

The events and characters contained in this book are of course fictitious. Unfortunately the theme is not. The business of sex slave trafficking of young innocent girls should concern us all. It has become a National and International crime that grows daily.

The facts and statistics referred to and quoted by characters in this book surrounding this crime against humanity are real.

Toward the end of this book's writing a real life event occurred in Nigeria where over two hundred and seventy Christian school girls were kidnapped by an Islamic extremist organization calling itself Boca Haram. Any semblance of this actual event and what you are about to read is absolute coincidence and taken by literary license by the author.

It is, however, the intent and hope of the author that the publishing of this book may raise some attention and action against the hideous and dehumanizing crime of sex slave trafficking and bring some relief to its' victims.

Author's Note: To readers who have struggled through my previous books and are bold enough to start this one, I ran across a quote this morning published by Philip Alder in his daily Bridge Column of my daily newspaper that may be of some help for you;

"Randy K. Milholland, the creator of several web comics, said, 'Typos are very important to all written form. It gives the reader something to look to so he isn't distracted by the total lack of content in your writing.'"

I take total responsibility and plead guilty. My publisher does not edit any of my manuscripts. I might add to 'typos' in the quote above and include; mispeeling, grammatical and sentence structure errors. For these I cannot even blame on my poor typing skills. My only hope is that someday, I might be able to afford a legitimate editor. (Hmm, does 'that' belong in the last sentence? Oh where is Mr. Mitchell, my high school English teacher?)

PART I
Fun-Dee
Loose Thai translation; Dream, Hope

CHAPTER ONE

Choi Boonlian and Juidel Suttikul, two fifteen year old girls from Thailand, sat in the dark, dank and stinking fish hold of the rusty one hundred twenty foot trawler named in Thai, 'Neap Tide'. They sat shivering with their arms wrapped around each other for warmth and comfort among the twenty or so other girls.

The two girls had similar backgrounds, both the eldest daughters from poor village families and were twelve years old when they were brought to Bangkok by their parents and sold to the owners of a clothing manufacturer and taught to be seamstresses. They were clothed, provided room and board and paid the equivalent of seventy-five cents for a twelve hour work day.

Working and living side by side for the past two years, they had developed a deep friendship and love for one another. On their one day off a week, while visiting the market place, they were confronted by a friendly Caucasian couple. The woman appeared matronly and sincere and spoke Thai. She explained to them that the man accompanying her was a rich client from America and was looking for domestic help to return with him to the United States.

She showed them pictures of the man's large estate that was located next to a lake with beautiful surroundings of evergreen trees and mountains. She also showed them pictures of the maid chambers and promised them a salary of five hundred dollars a month, keep, and only a five day work week.

The two young girls couldn't contain their excitement and good fortune. The only problem was, the woman explained, the gentleman was due to board his cruise ship that afternoon for his return journey and if they accepted they would have to join them now. She assured them they would be provided with clothing and supplies from the ship's store.

Choi looked at Juidel and giggled, "What do we have to lose. Let's do it."

They were escorted and put into the back seat of a luxury sedan and they again marveled at their good fortune as they rubbed their hands along the suede lining. The sun was setting behind them when they approached the port and their eyes opened wide when they saw the huge ocean going cruise ship moored next to the pier.

"Is that the ship we'll travel on?" Juidel asked in awe.

The lady turned to look at them and smiled, "Yes, it is."

Choi pinched herself to make sure she wasn't dreaming and whispered to Juidel, "When we get to America, I'll call you Judith and you can call me Joy."

The sedan passed by the cruise ship and pulled into an industrial park and parked next to a warehouse.

"You'll have to wait here for an hour or so with the other girls, until it's time to board," the lady said, helping them out of the back seat.

They entered through a door into the building and found themselves in a room with about two dozen other girls and it was abuzz with giggling and frolicking. The girls were all sitting in fold up chairs in a classroom like arrangement and a large Asian man sat at a desk in front of them. The lady assigned each girl a chair and walked up to the man at the desk and they spoke briefly. The man opened the center desk drawer and withdrew two envelopes and handed them to her. As the lady turned and walked past the girls toward the door she said, "Good luck girls."

Two hours later the girls were ushered out into the now dark night and loaded into a bus. They were driven out onto a dock and off loaded next to a fishing trawler. They were told it was the taxi boat that would take them to the cruise ship.

While being led aboard, Choi turned to her friend and said, "I think we need traveling papers for this. Maybe we'll get them on the cruise ship."

Juidel whispered, "Maybe this wasn't such a good idea."

Once on board, the girls were led by the large Asian man to a double opened hatch on the fore deck with a ladder that descended into the bowels of the boat. The first girl in line balked when she was ordered to climb down the ladder and the large man slapped her hard across her face and yelled, "Go, now!"

He turned to the rest of the girls and roared, "You will all do as you're told and you will not complain. Do you understand?"

A girl toward the end of the line whirled around and started to run towards the gang plank and was promptly subdued by a deck hand. She was dragged back across the deck to the large Asian man who said, "Take her to my cabin."

The other girls obeyed his command and climbed down the ladder into the dimly lit hold. Crude and soiled mattresses were strewn about the floor and a rusty sink and open commode sat in one corner. The stink in the room reminded the girls of the smell at the clothing plant when the wind shifted and carried the odors from the nearby garbage dump and open sewer, only worse.

Some of the girls were whimpering and some just sat in silence as the large double door slammed shut above them. An hour later the double doors opened again and the girl who had tried to escape was ordered back down the ladder. Her clothing had been torn and her exposed skin revealed cuts and bruises. She held her chin down and stumbled to a corner of the room and like a shamed puppy curled up in a ball.

They heard the motors of ship start up and a few minutes later they felt the vibration and loud hum when the propellers were engaged and the boat began moving. Over the next several weeks all of the girls experienced similar trips out of and several hours later back into the hold. No one spoke of the degrading acts they were forced to participate in.

Now, twenty days later, Choi and Juidel huddled together when the whirring clatter of the props stopped. The double doors opened and the large Asian man yelled, "Everybody out!"

As the girls, one by one, emerged from the fish hold they were blinded by the bright sun light and squinted their eyes and raised their hands to shield themselves from the glare. In turn, each girl was manacled by a wrist to a common rope.

"Hurry, they're getting closer," the large Asian man bellowed down from the wheel house.

With her eyes adjusted to the light, Choi looked frantically around, confused. She saw only the endless horizon of the ocean on all sides. Then she spotted the prow of another ship, which would turn out to be a U.S. Coast Guard Patrol cruiser, on the horizon steaming towards them. The line of girls, now all shackled to the rope, were led to the open boarding gate on the ships starboard side.

"What's happening?" Juidel asked.

Choi followed with her sad brown eyes to where the end of the rope rose and was latched to a large steel ball attached to the ship's davit. The crane was positioned at an angle over the ship's beam and above the choppy ocean. With horror she realized what was happening, but decided not to tell her friend. Instead, she buried her friends head in her bosom and whispered, "Just hang on to me. I love you Juidel."

The giant steel ball suddenly released and splashed into the ocean followed by the harrowing screams from the girls. Choi lost grip of her friend as they whipped off the side of the ship and were engulfed by the cold deep blue. Her final thoughts were those of her younger brothers and sisters at home.

CHAPTER TWO

The early evening breeze from the bay chilled the air and the ocean fog was just starting to roll in to encompass the Golden Gate Bridge and would soon bring its rainy mist to the City.

San Francisco District Attorney Chief Investigator Mary Dinosa stopped in front of the SFPD sawhorse blockade, a short distance from the end of Jefferson Street at Aquatic Park and rolled down her window. She produced her badge to the uniformed officer who then motioned to another uniformed officer who moved the barrier and Dinosa pulled forward.

Both sides of the street were lined with police cruisers and ambulances that extended all the way to the beach and dead ended at a turn-around adjacent to the beach. Another uniformed officer instructed her to park behind the SFPD Crime Scene Investigation van at the end of a long queue of official vehicles.

She grabbed her shoulder bag and a flash light and exited her car and started walking toward the beach with anxious feelings that this was going to be a bad one, mixed with the feelings of excitement of a new case. As she neared the beach she saw that flood lights had been set up at the end of Jefferson and the beach was dotted with similar lamps. A helicopter circled above and she noticed several Sheriff's Marine Department boats in the water.

"Hey Mary," she heard a familiar voice and turned to see her boss, District Attorney Valerie Kane, sitting in the back seat of a black sedan with the rear window rolled down.

She approached the car and said, "Jesus Val, since when did you respond to a crime scene?"

"Since eight dead women and still counting started drifting up on our beaches," Kane replied.

"Eight," Mary exclaimed perplexed, "I thought you said three?"

"That was when I talked to you last. Since then, they've found two more down the beach and three tangled up under the Jefferson Street Pier."

"What the hell happened?" Dinosa asked.

Kane shrugged and said, "Captain John Halfhide is on the beach and he's been keeping me updated, but so far all they can say is the bodies are extremely bloated and appear to be Asian women. They all have been dinner for the crabs and facial identification will be impossible."

"Who's the CSI?" Dinosa asked.

"It's Margaret Johnson and she's got her entire crew here," Kane answered.

"Thank God for that. How about the Homicide Inspector?"

"Halfhide assigned Marcus Jones and Frank Gardner. I know you just wrapped up the Doctor Davies' case, but I need you to stay on top of this one. God knows this will be a gigantic story," Kane said.

Kane leaned forward, nudged her driver on the shoulder and said, "Come on Pete, let's get out of here."

Dinosa spotted Marcus Jones and Frank Gardner standing together with Margaret Johnson on the beach sidewalk and joined them. Jones and Gardner were referred to in the department as the Mutt and Jeff team and one look at the pair would tell you why. Gardner stood six foot five inches tall and was thin as a rail with a bulging nose and Jones was a black man about five and half feet tall and almost as round.

Two CSI trainees were carrying a stretcher with a body bag on it up from the beach. Johnson stopped them and unzipped the bag, exposing the victims face. Most of the skin and meat had been removed revealing the woman's open jaw and teeth.

With a pen light, Johnson examined her teeth and commented, "Same as the others. What little dental work they've had done wasn't done in this country."

She unzipped the bag a little farther until she could observe the shackle biting into her bloated wrist.

Turning toward the other three she said, "I can't say for sure, but I'd bet my left tit, the coroner will determine the cause of death as asphyxiation due to drowning. The three we salvaged from the pier pilings still had the rope binding them together."

"Jesus Christ, these women were shackled together and thrown overboard somewhere. Do we have any idea where?" Dinosa asked.

"The Port Authority, the Coast Guard and the Sheriff's Marine Unit are together right now examining charts and trying to determine where they may have been dumped. The Port Authority Commander did say that the tides have been extremely high and the currents strong and says it'll be hard to pin point where they were dumped," Gardner commented.

"He also said an approximate time of death would be helpful, but we'll have to wait for the Coroner's report," Jones added.

Dinosa looked at Johnson and asked, "Do we know what age these girls were?"

"Well, the coroner will be able to tell us more, but based on the bone structure and pelvic development on those I've examined, I'd guess there are several pre-puberty and the others from twelve to early teens," Johnson answered.

"I think, for now, we should work under the assumption that these girls were smuggled here for the purpose of illegal sex. Let's get the Sex Crimes Unit involved and start hitting up all the known massage parlors, escort services and strip joints that feature Asian girls," Dinosa said and added, "Let's rattle some cages, no I take that back, let's fucking blow some cages up and see what we can find."

Bernard Rusk sat in his office behind his desk at CIA Headquarters in Langley, Virginia. It was just past midnight, Eastern Standard Time, and he was on the phone with his boss, the Director, and simultaneously monitoring his computer screen and real time reports coming in from his San Francisco field office. Rusk was the Deputy Director of ICA, International Criminal Activity and Homeland Security for the CIA. That was his official title, but his unofficial persona and power far exceeded his official title.

"Yes Sir, I'm sure this will trace this back to the T'Siang Society," he told his boss.

After hanging up, he leaned back in his chair, raised his arms, rested his head on folded hands and closed his eyes. Several moments later, he sat upright and dialed a number on his secure telephone.

"Hey George, it's Bernie…Yeah, as a matter of fact I'm monitoring the events as they unfold which brings me to why I'm calling. We're going to need you and the Justice Foundation's help. Do you think you can get the group together by tomorrow at the O'Farrell residence?… Great, and one more favor, could you have the lovely Ms. Dinosa pick me up around eleven am. I'll be arriving by helicopter at Crissy Field…Oh, between you and Ian I'm sure you can talk her into it. Thanks, George."

After his conversation with Bernard Rusk, George Armstrong leaned back in his chair and reflected on his relationship with his friend that began over forty years ago. It started with a phone call from Rusk when Armstrong was a young and successful criminal lawyer with his practice in San Jose, California. He had recently notched victories in several high profile murder cases and credited much of his success to his early association with Bernard Rusk.

Rusk, after completing several tours in Viet Nam with the CIA as a young Special Ops Agent and after resigning his position with the agency, had accepted a position at the Harvard School of Law as an assistant professor. Although the two had yet to meet each other at the time, by reputation they were well aware of the others achievement. In a relative short period of time, Rusk had earned his full professorship and came to be called 'Los Santos', a nickname afforded him by a young South American student that translated in English to 'the Saint'.

He had called Armstrong to ask for a favor. A Sergeant in the Army Special Forces he had met and became close to when he was attached to the Sergeant's unit in Viet Nam had a younger brother in the Santa Clara County jail charged with rape and a double murder. The brother was being represented by a public defender and the Sergeant had reached out to him for help. He now asked Armstrong if he would just look into it.

When Armstrong called the P.D. and the man didn't even recognize the defendant's name, he decided to delve into the matter further and it didn't take him long to become convinced the D.A.'s charges were bogus. He agreed to take the case pro bono if Rusk would take second chair. Together they got the kid off and the short trial was the beginning of a lifelong friendship.

Five year ago, Armstrong's widowed mother, a philanthropist and a member of several nonprofit organizations board of directors, was shot and killed by a notorious serial killer in San Francisco. The murderer was targeting mostly successful and well off women in the city. Together with several other family members of the killer's victims they formed the 'Justice Foundation' whose sole purpose at the time was to ensure this killer met the justice he deserved.

After almost a year and a half passed and the serial killer had still not been captured, they recruited the original SFPD Homicide Inspector on the case, the now retired Chuck Chalmers, as a private investigator. One of the Justice Foundation's members, Sean O'Farrell and the husband of one of the killer's first victims, had a son, Ian O'Farrell, a former team commander of a Navy Seal team.

Chalmers discovered the identity and the diabolical motive of the serial killer and with Ian O'Farrell and several of Ian's former Seal team members they traced and followed the killer to an island in the Caribbean.

By this time Sean's old friend had returned to the CIA and had climbed the clandestine organization's power ladder. He now called on his old friend's resources in tracing the killer's location. Bernie was happy to help.

George thought that was the beginning of some wild rides over the past few years and it appears has led them to the start of another.

Rusk, still at his desk, dialed another number and said, "Gary, its Bernard. I need you to meet me in San Francisco tomorrow morning at eleven fifteen…Yeah, the usual place and thanks."

Gary Brown was an off the books, deep cover CIA Agent. Rusk had recruited him while Brown was a fourth year cadet at West Point, majoring in Linguistics and Computer Sciences fifteen years ago. He was fluent speaking several languages including Arabic, Farsi, Thai, Spanish and both Chinese dialects. He was also a powerful physical specimen and after graduating from the Academy he completed Army Ranger training and led CIA black operations in Iraq, Afghanistan and Somalia.

He was an only child and lost his parents in a car accident during his first year at West Point. Two years ago his surviving Grandparents were informed he was missing in action while on patrol in Afghanistan and to the world he disappeared. Rusk resurrected him with his new name and identity as a freelance travel log journalist and Rusk was one of the few people who knew his true identity. Since his reincarnation he had participated in covert operations and his contributions were always anonymous. He received his orders and answered to Bernard Rusk only.

"What, you want me to drop everything in the middle of the murder investigation of eight young girls to play chauffeur for that arrogant asshole Bernard Rusk?" Dinosa hollered at her fiancé Ian O'Farrell as she wiggled into her suit pants.

"All I can tell you is that George Armstrong called me this morning and requested that you pick up Mr. Rusk and drive him to my Dad's place and it has something to do with your investigation. You know how helpful Rusk has been in the past, so it could contribute to your investigation," Ian calmly explained and added, "He wants to meet with the Foundation and you. Hey, it's your decision."

"Jesus, I hate spooks," Dinosa moaned.

"Does that mean I'll meet you at Dad's around noon?" he asked.

"Yes, alright yes," Dinosa replied frustrated.

She finished dressing, clipped her sidearm to her hip and looking around the bedroom she groaned, "Ah Christ, where did I put my keys?"

"Try the kitchen counter," Ian laughed.

"Oh, so you think this is funny? I can't wait until we move into the new house so I can find things," she said angrily as she grabbed her keys off of the counter and stomped out.

She was still fuming when she hit a slow, stop and go traffic jam at Market Street. She honked her horn at the driver in front of her when he stopped at a yellow light and mumbled to herself, "You fucking idiot, we both could have made it."

She repeated the serenity prayer she had learned from her former Homicide partner, Chuck Chalmers, during a particularly difficult case. 'God, grant me the serenity to accept the things I cannot change.'

She started reviewing her plan for the day that was already screwed up with this Bernard Rusk bull shit. As lead investigator of the task force she would be responsible for Homicide and Sex Crime officer assignments and coordinating the efforts of the Coast Guard, the Port Authority and the Sheriff's Marine detail and liaison with the District Attorney. And now she had to baby sit that asshole Rusk.

"Fuck!" she groaned.

Finally arriving at SFPD Head Quarters at 850 Bryant Street, she parked in the adjacent parking lot and hustled up to the fourth story Homicide offices. She was met at the front desk by Florence Valstead, the civilian office manager.

"Your task force has been assigned the same conference room you had for the Davie's case," Florence stated and handing her a stack of folders she added, "These are the preliminary autopsy reports from Dr. Zoeller and I put the combined Coast Guard and Port Authority report on your desk in the conference room."

"Thanks Flo, and would you please get the Coast Guard Commander, the Port Authority Commander and the Captain of the Sheriff's Marine Unit on the phone and request they attend a meeting for three o'clock this afternoon?"

Picking up and dialing her phone, Florence said, "Yes, Ma'am."

When Dinosa walked into the conference room she was greeted by Marcus Jones and two people she didn't recognize. Jones introduced Inspector's Bud Paulus and Ramona Vasquez from Sex Crimes. Bud Paulus was a short, stocky sandy haired man with an unkempt beard she guessed to be in his early thirties. Ramona Vasquez was a petite, attractive Latino woman in her late twenties.

Frank Gardner walked into the room and introductions were made. The group took seats around a table located at one end of the room.

"Okay," Dinosa started, looking at Paulus and Vasquez, "We are proceeding under the assumption that these girls were being illegally transported here by sex traders, so we're going to come down hard on their potential places of work.

"Can you provide us with a list with addresses of all the massage parlors, strip clubs, escort services, pimps, and any other place you can think of that would possibly hire illegals?"

Vasquez reached into her shoulder bag and produced a folder. "We anticipated you'd want this. It's a list of all the places you just mentioned that our department has compiled."

"This is great. I'll get these over to the D.A. and get search and arrest warrants. We'd like to hit these places as soon as possible. I've reserved the Police Gymnasium as an assembly area for those we arrest. This has to be a coordinated effort and I suggest you two do the planning. You'll have the number of uniforms and transport you believe necessary. Keep in mind, this has to be done soon."

"There are thirteen names and addresses on that list. I propose we assign each location to a Sex Crime officer and at least two uniforms. It would be best to hit the massage parlors and the escort services in the early morning when business should be light. Some of the escort services are advertised by a telephone number only, but we have the addresses of the dispatchers, who are usually fairly innocuous women, making a few extra dollars working out of their homes. A lot of the call girls work the strip joints at night, so the ones we don't get we can tag that evening. The street pimps will have to be picked up as we find them," Paulus said.

"What about the Johns we find?" Vasquez asked.

"I want them all, the Johns, the hookers, the pimps, the madams, the managers, the receptionists, the dispatchers and the bouncers. Hell, I even want the bartenders and janitors. When we have them, we're going to squeeze them all," Dinosa spitted out squeezing her hand into a fist.

"I hope you realize the political repercussions this action will probably incur. I've been working Vice and Sex Crimes Detail long enough to know some of our City's finest citizens frequent these places and most of the establishment owners have a lot of political pull. We'll be opening a Pandora's box," Paulus commented.

"I don't give a shit," Dinosa pontificated, "We're going to turn this City upside down and shake it and when the shit falls out, they're going to cooperate or we're going to prosecute. I don't care where these dead little girls came from or what their backgrounds are, they didn't deserve to die this way and they deserve justice!"

Dinosa was shaking and she questioned the motivation of her passion. No, she thought, I'm justified with my outrage. How many other innocent young girls have suffered the same fate to fulfill the perverted needs of some men, and even worse, to line the pockets of some of the world's sickest people? It's not going to continue to happen in her City.

She lowered her voice and lied, "I've discussed this with my boss, D.A. Valerie Kane, and she gives her one hundred percent support."

"If I can make a suggestion," Vasquez interrupted and continued, "I think, for the sake of credibility and to cover our asses, that all of the raiding officers wear helmet or lapel cams during the operations."

"That's an excellent idea, and it brings to mind one other thing. As of now, only the people in this room and Valerie Kane know about this operation. Let's keep it that way. Does anybody have an excuse we can use to explain transportation, reserving the gym and our man power request?"

"When I worked Vice Detail, we would occasionally conduct City wide dragnets to bust organized and gang related drug busts and they would require similar inter department cooperation. We can delay briefing our team leaders as to the true nature of the operation until the last minute," Gardner said.

Dinosa looked around the room and seeing no objection she said, "Okay, we'll go with that. These girls were lured here with the hope and promise that they might realize the American dream and, like our forefathers, they were willing to work to achieve that goal. They experienced the American nightmare.

"Last night I Googled the English translation for the Thai word for 'dream' and it said 'fun-dee'. To honor these girls, we're going to call our effort 'Operation Fun-dee'. Tomorrow morning we kick it off, so let's get to work."

She glanced at her wrist watch and noticed the time was nine forty-five am, and she realized she had one more important task before she met Rusk and this too, she didn't look forward to. She had to meet with her boss and get approval for something she had already put in motion.

Ten minutes later she arrived at City Hall and knocked on the opened door of Valerie Kane's Office and when Kane acknowledged her, she entered, sat down on the chair adjacent to the desk and produced two file folders from her shoulder bag.

She handed them to Kane and said, "The first file is an updated report on the Aquatic Park case and our plan to execute 'Operation Fun-dee'. The second file contains the names and places of known illegal sex outlets that we will need search warrants for, and John and Jane Doe arrest warrants for anyone found on the premises for operating, employed by or frequenting a known illegal establishment."

Kane looked at Dinosa shaking her head and said, "Mary you never cease to amaze me. Why don't you just tell me what's in this report?"

Dinosa explained the operation and concluded by saying, "Oh, I'll need your approval and the warrants by this evening, but no later than first thing tomorrow morning and we need to keep this hush, hush."

Looking down and again shaking her head, Kane groaned, "And I suppose, if I agree to this and I procure your warrants, you can assure me there won't be any repercussions?"

"Nope," Dinosa replied and looking at her wrist watch she added, "Oh shit, I've got to go."

The wind had whipped up some and white caps covered the Bay waters as Dinosa pulled up and parked next to the West Bluff Amphitheater at Crissy Field on Marine Drive just as the helicopter was setting down on the grassy knoll in front of her. The side chopper door opened and its lone passenger hopped out and started jogging toward her. The helicopter lifted and swung out over the Bay.

Watching Rusk trot across the field, Dinosa marveled at the physical condition of this octogenarian old fart and wondered what kept the old man going. She inwardly admired his dedication to serving his country and his silent accomplishments over the years since he was a young buck conducting black ops in Viet Nam. He possessed honesty and humility about him that she was sure could charm a Nun out of her habit.

He opened the passenger side door, slid in beside her and slightly out of breath said, "Mary, it's so good to see you again. How have you been?"

She couldn't resist leaning across the seat and kissing him on his cheek, "Just fine, thank you. I suppose you want me to chauffeur you to Sean O'Farrell's place in Sausalito?"

"No, but thank you for the offer. If you could drive to the end of Marine Drive and indulge me in a little conversation, I'd appreciate it," he replied and then reaching into his valise and pulling out a bottle of wine, he added, "Oh, before I forget, I've brought you and Ian a pre-wedding gift. It's a bottle of Colgin Cellars '96 Cabernet Sauvignon."

"Thank you Bernie and I'm sure Ian will enjoy it, but you should know I can't tell the difference between a fine wine and a bottle of ripple."

They drove along the bay's shoreline and came to the turnaround parking lot under the Golden Gate Bridge at Fort Point. Rusk handed her a thumb drive and said, "This may help you in your current investigation. It contains satellite imagery of your crime scene. Those poor girls were dumped into the sea off the deck of a Thai fishing trawler just before they were to be boarded by the U.S. Coast Guard."

Dinosa parked the car and taking the thumb drive, she said excitingly, "Oh Bernie, this is great! Where did this happen?"

"Just a few miles south of the Farallon Islands. It seems they had trouble with their GPS and the skipper's explanation was, they thought they were one hundred miles north and two hundred miles west looking for schools of Tuna fish. The girls were dumped at ten forty-six a.m., three days ago and according to our analysts the El Nino current and the tides would have carried the bodies to your beach, if the anchor rope broke."

"Is the name of the boat visible?" Dinosa asked with anticipation.

"Better than that, we believe we have the name of the boat they were supposed to meet to transfer their cargo. The name of the trawler is 'Neap Tide' out of Thailand and the boat that was mysteriously steaming toward them and suddenly made a U-turn is called 'Buddha Rules', which is conflicting since Buddha is considered a very benevolent Deity."

He reached into his valise, produced an envelope and handing it to an open mouthed Dinosa, said, "Here, this is a report that includes the name and address of the registered owners of the sixty foot yacht called 'Buddha Rules'."

"Son of a bitch, Bernie," Dinosa almost giggled, "I take back all of the bad things I've said about you."

"What's that supposed to mean?" Rusk feigned innocence.

"Never mind, just thank you, thank you, thank you," and she reached over and hugged the old fart.

"Well, I've got to run, but if I should come across anything else that might help you, I'll pass it on," Rusk said, opening the door and stepping out into the brisk wind.

"Thanks again," Dinosa hollered after him as she watched him cross the parking lot and climb into the passenger seat of a black SUV.

—

"It's good to see you, Gary," Rusk said reaching across the seat and shaking Brown's hand. "I've got a new job for you."

Gary Brown intentionally presented himself in appearance as a forty year old aging intellectual and effeminate type. He wore wide brimmed glasses unnecessarily, as his vision was twenty-twenty, and loose fitting clothes that camouflaged his fit and well-defined body.

His father was a retired U.S. Army Colonel and met his mother, a Thai woman and Medical Doctor, while on R and R leave in Thailand from his duties in Viet Nam. After they married they took up residence in the Seattle, Washington area, and raised their only son before their untimely deaths.

"It's good to see you too, sir. It's been a little boring parading as a travel log journalist," Brown replied.

Brown as a journalist was known as William Gray, and it allowed him to travel around the world fairly inconspicuously. He was occasionally published in travel periodicals, but had never authored any of them. His ghost writer was actually a woman who worked in the Special Operations Division at the CIA.

"Since I know where we're going, I should drive," Rusk said and they traded places.

"We're going to the home of Sean O'Farrell and you're going to meet a group of individuals you haven't met before, but you are familiar with. Several years ago you tagged a drone target on an island off Greece. The 'Justice Foundation' was in part responsible for that operation and you're about to meet them," Rusk said.

"Hum, interesting," Brown replied simply.

Handing him a folder marked 'Top Secret', Rusk continued, "Here's the report and proposal I'm going to present to them. While I'm driving, I want you to read it."

They drove across the Golden Gate Bridge in silence and took the Sausalito exit. The route wound down the hill overlooking the small coastal town and after making several switchback turns, Rusk pulled in to a lane and up to a remote controlled gate. He lowered his window and looked up and smiled at the camera. The gate raised and

Rusk proceeded to drive up along the tree lined lane. After making a lazy left turn the impressive O'Farrell Mansion came into view.

"Wow," Brown remarked.

Rusk parked the vehicle below the stairs that led up to the manor's entrance and they exited the SUV. At the top of the stairs was Ian O'Farrell waving them up.

When they met at the top landing, Rusk was about to introduce the two when Ian said, "Holy Mary Mother of God, is that you Gary Brown? I heard you were KIA years ago."

"Hey, Colonel O'Farrell, it's good to see you. You can call me Mark Twain and the news of my demise was greatly exaggerated." Brown said with a beaming smile.

As the two embraced in a hug, Rusk said, "I should have known you two would have met before."

"Yeah, and the rumor of your demise was slightly exaggerated. Come on in," Ian laughed.

Ian led them through the entrance and to the den where Ian's father Sean along with George Armstrong and Solomon Goldsmith rose to greet them.

After Brown was introduced to the group and all were seated, Rusk started, "I'm sure we can all agree this is a sad day in our nation's history. The young ladies that washed up on your shores yesterday started their journey with the hope of realizing the American dream. The fact that they would have been illegal immigrants in no way justifies neither their fate nor the sons of bitches that lured them here for financial gain.

"Had they successfully reached land alive, let me tell you what awaited them. We've learned from intelligence reports this particular group of girls were recruited because of their youth and beauty by a powerful and extremely secretive group called the T'Siang Society. They're headquartered in Hong Kong.

"These girls, we believe, were to be sold either as a group or individually to sex traders in the Bay Area. They would have been provided with counterfeit papers that their new owners would hold, and placed in massage parlors or sold to individuals to be used as sex slaves. As prostitutes in the whore houses they would be told they would have to turn tricks to pay off the forty to fifty thousand dollar passage fare. The house would receive anywhere from one hundred to two hundred dollars per trick and the girls would be credited ten dollars for each trick they performed.

"Do the math and try to determine how long it would take to work off their debt. Then consider the conditions these girls would live in. If they revolted in any way they would be savagely beaten as an example. If one of them managed to escape, they would be hunted down and mysteriously never seen again."

Rusk paused and took a large gulp from his water glass and continued, "The sale of illicit sex slaves has become a world-wide epidemic. It now ranks third, behind the illegal narcotics and illegal arms trades, in global revenue.

"We have partnered with several European countries and Interpol to combat this epidemic. Unfortunately, most of this underworld network has its roots in China and Russia, two nations where covert operations on our part is very dicey to say the least."

He handed Sean the 'Top Secret' file and said, "This is my report and proposal to you. Perhaps you can make enough copies so you each get one to review and discuss in private. In the meantime Gary and I will tour your town. By the way, is that place called the 'Crab Shack' still in operation?"

Ian chuckled and said, "It sure is and in the same place, but I warn you Gary, it's addictive."

"When we return, I'll have to collect your copies of the report and burn them. I know it sounds a little Bondish, but that is the original and only copy in existence. You've got my number so please call when you're ready for us to return."

—

When Dinosa arrived back in the conference room at 850 Bryant Street she assembled the team and said, "I've been given a video I think we all should see."

She plugged in the thumb drive to the console operating the large screen monitor and asked Jones to dim the lights. A moment later the satellite image of a trawler sitting idle in the ocean appeared on the screen. The camera zoomed down and a group of young Asian girls could be clearly seen being led out of a hold and one by one shackled to a single rope attached to a large metallic ball hanging from the ship's davit. The girls were herded to the port side deck and the metallic ball was released.

Ramona Vasquez turned her head and moaned, "Oh my God."

Dinosa depressed the pause button on the remote and said, "Dammit, I want us all to watch this and realize the type of people we're dealing with. I'm going to continue the video in slow motion and I want each of us to count the number of girls going overboard so we have an accurate number of murders we'll have to charge these bastards."

She resumed the video in slow motion and the group of observers watched in horror as one by one the girls were yanked overboard and disappeared with a splash into the deep blue. Two girls near the middle of the group were embraced in a desperate hug and were violently torn apart when the slack in the rope became taut.

The camera rotated toward the ship's stern and below the ships name written in Thai were the words in English, 'Neap Tide' and 'Thailand'. Dinosa again froze the video and asked, "I counted twenty-five girls. Does that jive with everybody else?"

Everyone nodded and she resumed the video. The scene retracted up until the trawler could barely be seen. At the bottom of the screen a larger ship could be seen steaming toward the trawler from the southeast. At the top of the screen a smaller boat could be seen and from the arc of its wake it had made a U-turn and was heading back toward land. The camera zoomed in until the name of the boat could be clearly seen. It read, 'Buddha Rules', and underneath, 'San Francisco, CA'.

The camera followed the 'Buddha Rules' in fast forward and slowed to real time as it passed under the Golden Gate Bridge and then resumed in fast forward until the boat docked at a berth in the Saint Francis Yacht Club Marina in San Francisco.

"Son of a bitch," Jones remarked, "That's only a couple of blocks from where the girls washed up."

As the passengers debarked the camera zoomed in on them and showed five people. The first to step ashore was a slim Asian woman who appeared to be in her forties. She was followed ashore by a short almost obese, Asian man, then a tall good looking Caucasian man followed by two younger Asian men. The video flickered and then stopped.

The room was silent for several moments until Gardner spoke, "I think I recognize the fat Asian guy. If I'm right, I remember him from my days at Narcotics. His name is Billy Choo. He was a top lieutenant in the Wah Ching gang in Chinatown. He was suspected of being the king pin of an opium and heroin smuggling operation. He emigrated here with his parents and siblings from Cambodia shortly after the end of the Viet Nam war. Many of us thought the real mastermind of the operation was Joey Wang, head of the Huang Tong. It was an ongoing investigation when I transferred out and I understand we busted several of his underlings, but couldn't reach him."

"Okay Frank, you see if you can confirm his identity and his fellow passengers. Take this video to our IT people and see if they can enhance the video and get still shots of the Yacht's passengers and of the trawler's crew and the girls. I'm going to ask my boss if she can reach out to the State Department and see what can be done about detaining the 'Neap Tide' and the crew. I'm sure they're half way back to Thailand by now.

"Marcus, I need you to get down to the marina and observe that Yacht. I'll brief the Port Authority and have a Sheriff's boat standing by. If someone boards it and decides to take her out on a cruise, I want you and the Sheriff's craft to follow them. I don't think we can show enough cause to detain this Billy Choo and his fellow passengers, but we might be able to attain a warrant to seize and search the boat.

"Ramona and Bud, you guys make sure all the arrangements for Operation Fun-Dee are in place and ready to go by tomorrow morning."

Approximately an hour after they each were handed a copy of the 'Top Secret' documents from Rusk to be given the opportunity to individually read and study it, George Armstrong commented, "It seems to me this is another off the books operation Rusk wants us to undertake and cover the CIA's ass. I'm not saying this is necessarily wrong' as we've done it before, but this one looks like an extremely dangerous proposition."

"I agree this would be a very dangerous mission, but the report tells us more than twenty-five million young girls worldwide are currently the direct victims of this atrocious enterprise. Speaking for myself, and I'm not going to be the one in harm's way, I think it's a worthy cause. However," he continued, looking at Ian, "I think before we make a decision we should have the input from members of Ian's team."

Glancing at his father and Armstrong and getting no negative response, Ian said, "I'll fetch Jesse and Grant. I think they're in the gym. Dad, see if you can get Steve and Nancy on Skype."

Ian left the room and made his way to the home's basement gymnasium. The room was large with a hand-to-hand combat mat on one end of the floor adjacent to a state-of-the-art workout area and a boxing ring. The far end of the room was dedicated to a regulation sized half-court basketball court. A two lane, one eighth mile long running catwalk positioned sixteen feet above the floor circled the room.

Jesse Leone and Grant Wilson were playing one-on-one basketball. They were both former members of an elite Navy Seal's Team commanded by Ian O'Farrell and were recruited several years ago by Ian to pursue and capture the serial murderer of Ian's mother.

That mission was financed by his father and several other surviving husbands of victims of the same serial killer and led to the formation of the 'Justice Foundation'. The board members consisted of the men upstairs and Ian who also led the field operations team. Jesse and Grant resided in the home as active members of that team and Steve and Nancy Cromwell, also former members of Ian's Seal Team, remained on stand-by at their ski resort located in the northern end of the State. The field team members were all in their early thirties with the exception of Ian who was thirty-six.

Jesse Leone, an American Latino, was about five feet, seven inches tall and his muscles had muscles. Ian respected him as the strongest pound for pound man he had ever met. Grant Wilson was a black man and his muscular body stood well over six foot tall. Both men sported military style high and tight hair-cuts.

"Hey guys," Ian hollered across the room, "You're presence is requested upstairs."

Jesse was in possession of the basketball and they both stopped and looked over at Ian. Jesse then darted around the much bigger man and made a lay-up.

"Ha, ha, that makes it eleven to ten, I win!" he laughed.

"You little prick, you cheated!" Grant roared with mock anger.

They walked over to Ian, Grant limping slightly from a healing bullet wound to his left leg sustained in their last mission. Over half of this right ear was missing and scabbed over as a result of another wound from the same mission.

"How's the leg?" Ian asked as they walked toward the stairwell.

"Almost back to normal. When it is, this little prick won't stand a chance on that basketball court," Grant replied.

"What's going on with the ear?" Ian inquired.

"I'm supposed to have reconstructive surgery next week."

"Why don't you see if they can do anything with that ugly mug?" Jesse chuckled.

When they reached the den they were heartily greeted by Sol and George who inquired about Grants' wounds. Steve and Nancy were displayed on the large screen monitor and exchanged greetings and similar concerns.

Grant mumbled, "I'm doing fine."

"He goes in for reconstructive surgery next week," Jesse commented and added, "They're going to make a woman out of him."

The comment elicited laughs from everyone and a dirty look from Grant.

"Here's the deal," Ian began.

A half hour later, he concluded, "I believe you all remember Gary Brown. He was the lead man and collected the intel on that operation to rescue the missionary family we extracted that were being held by that asshole war lord in Somalia."

"I thought he was KIA in Afghanistan?" Steve remarked.

"That's how good he is. He's been dark since then and he'll be our front man in Hong Kong," Ian said and added, "And except for cooperation from a corrupt Hong Kong Deputy Police Commissioner and our Embassy to give us cover, we'll be pretty much on our own."

Nancy looked at Steve who gave her a nod and she said, "We've all seen what these people do and the wrecked lives they leave behind here and overseas. If we can do something to help stop it, count us in."

"If we wait until after Grant's surgery, we can insert him in as a hooker mole," Jesse snickered.

"Fuck you, Leone. Yeah, we're in," Grant said.

"Okay Nancy and Steve, as soon as we've developed an operational plan we'll send you an encrypted email. In the meantime, enjoy the slopes and be ready to move," Ian said, cutting off the Skype feed.

Gary Brown turned toward Rusk as they were waiting for the gate to the O'Farrell estate to open and said, "Do you think they'll accept?"

"I think you'll be flying to Hong Kong and Ian and his team will be following you there shortly," Rusk replied with a smile.

—

"Hey Snoopy, Mary Dinosa here, how's little Pig Pen doing?" She said into the phone.

Snoopy was the nickname for Belinda Grant, a former member of the Computer Forensic Investigation Unit at SFPD, who was married to Daniel Tanaka, known to his friends as Grub because of his scruffy dress and appearance. Grub was respected as one of the most qualified computer engineers and scientists in the world and the two had met when he was called in as a consultant to help investigate the 'North Beach Serial Killer' by the Justice Foundation. They subsequently married, had a baby a year ago, and started their own computer consulting firm. Their services had been hired frequently by the City of San Francisco, the Justice Department and the CIA over the past several years.

"Oh, Danny Junior is doing just great. Grub swears he heard him say 'papa' the other day, but I think it was just baby talk. What can we do for you?" Snoopy replied.

Dinosa asked if Grub was there and Snoopy called him over and put the call on speaker. She then briefed them on the case and concluded, "We're convinced that Billy Choo and Joey Wang are the leaders of the people bringing these girls in, but so far we haven't been able pin anything on them that would stand up in a court of law. We need to follow the money and that's where you two come in to play. What do you need?"

"Let me write this down," Grub paused and then continued, "You say the name is the Huang Tong led by Joey Wang and it's the Wah Ching gang led by Billy Choo?"

"Yes," Dinosa replied.

"And the name of the company owned by Ronald and Roselyn Bingham is called Asian Import, Ltd?'

"Yep," Dinosa answered.

"That's all we need for now," Grub said.

"You guys are amazing. You'll be hearing from Ian and Bernie Rusk. I believe they're going after the international culprits and, by the way, include the work you're doing for us on your bill to the Justice Foundation and thank you," Dinosa concluded and hung up.

Gardner entered the room and plopped a handful of pictures on Dinosa's desk and said, "These are the stills of everyone on board the

'Buddha Rules'. I was right, the fat guy is Billy Choo. The white guy is Ronald Bingham and the Asian woman is his wife Roselyn. They are the owners of 'Asian Imports, Ltd.' A British Corporation. The two younger Asian men are known members of the Wah Ching gang. I should be getting the criminal and background sheets on all of them soon."

"That's great," Dinosa said and added, "Get copies of these pictures to Bud and Ramona to hand out to all of the team leaders and see if you can help them out. We need to make sure 'Operation Fun-Dee' goes down without a hitch."

She picked up the phone and dialed Ian's number.

"Hey Babe, it's me. Are you still with Bernard Rusk?" she asked.

"Yeah, we're just breaking up our meeting," Ian replied.

"Good, can you put him on and ah, I'll probably be a little late for dinner tonight," she said.

"That's okay, I was going to call you to tell you I won't be home tonight and probably for quite some time. We've got a mission. Hang on and I'll get Bernie," Ian said.

After a moment Rusk came on and said, "Hey Mary, what's up?"

"I was hoping you'd have the time to meet with Valerie Kane and me this afternoon or early this evening," Dinosa requested.

"I can manage that. How about we meet in Valerie's office in a couple of hours?" Rusk replied.

Dinosa glanced at her watch and said, "Six o'clock then," and hung up.

—

CHAPTER THREE

The Hong Kong International Commerce Centre Building in West Kowloon sat on an entire city block and stood eighty-eight stories high. It was one of the tallest buildings in Hong Kong, but the construction cranes atop taller structures that dotted the high rise eastern landscape indicated its reputation would soon be diminished.

Chow Gai, Chief Executive Officer and President of Asian Exports Ltd., the sister Company of Asian Imports, Ltd., sat at his desk in a luxurious corner office on the eighty-first floor. He was reading an encrypted e-mail from his brother-in-law, Ronald Bingham. It was a report on the recent accident and the tragic loss estimated to be worth over two hundred thousand dollars.

As he read the report and rubbed his chin he contemplated not the monetary loss, but how it would affect future business and if he should consider making a change in shipment methods.

—

Upon concluding her briefing of the case to Valerie Kane in the D.A.'s office, Dinosa said, "We know who the main players are and it'll just be a matter of hard work and time to nail them, but we're going to need the help of the Feds. That's why I invited Bernard Rusk here. He should arrive any moment."

As if on cue, there was a knock on the door and Kane's Assistant ushered Bernard Rusk in.

Kane rose and hugged her one time Law Professor and mentor. "Oh Bernard, it's so good to see you again."

"It's good to see you too, Valerie," Rusk smiled and looking at Dinosa continued, "I don't have a lot of time, what can I do for you?"

"I don't need to know why you're in town, but I wanted to thank you for the information you provided Mary. Now we need your advice. It looks like, if we're going to prosecute Joey Wang and Ronald Bingham, we're going to need the Feds help. I doubt we will be able to tie them directly to the murders of these girls, but we're working on developing Rico charges. How can you help?" Valerie asked bluntly.

"Hmm, I taught you well. Let me think about that and you can expect a call tomorrow," Rusk replied.

After Rusk departed, Dinosa said, "You know Val, I've been thinking a lot about prostitution and the sex trade thing, and I've done some research on the subject and even though I have some mixed feeling, I've made some conclusions."

Kane dropped her jaw in mock horror and then said, "That's okay, Mary. Many women have fantasized about being a lady of the night."

"Damn it, Val, you know that's not what I meant," Dinosa groaned and continued, "Statistics tell us that illegal prostitution is by far the leading factor for the transmission of STDs, sexual assaults, rapes and murders and drug use by prostitutes is the highest of any of society's factions. The international sex trade commerce ranks only third behind the illegal drugs and arms trade in revenue. It's estimated over twenty million young girls world-wide are being forced into this industry. You should hear some of their stories.

"Some of them haven't even reached puberty. Their living conditions are deplorable and the sadistic acts they're forced to participate in, goes beyond despicable. Even in this Country, young run-aways and girls who've got mixed up with the wrong crowd have been snatched up by punk prick pimps and forced into this life style."

"What are you trying to say?" Kane asked.

"Well, I'm not so naïve that I believe we can put an end to this, but we can sure do something about it in our City. In Nevada Counties where prostitution is legal, these problems are practically nonexistent. The prostitutes are registered and willing participants. They are regularly tested for STDs and the premises are routinely inspected.

The owners and proprietors must be licensed and back ground investigations are performed. Tough laws against illegal activity are vigorously prosecuted and violators face stiff prison sentences. If there's one city in the United States that could follow their example, it would be San Francisco and you're the person to lead the crusade," Dinosa replied.

"As a matter of fact Mary, you've just echoed my sentiments and I have been doing something about it. I believe we have the support of the majority of city council members on our side and this latest event will probably sway our fence sitting Mayor to our side.

"You just concentrate on the investigation and I'll work on the politics. I agree we can make a difference in our City and maybe it will spread nation-wide. I think Bernard Rusk can help with that effort," Kane concluded.

"You're right and I should be getting back to my job," Dinosa said rising to leave.

When she reached the door, Kane stopped her and said, "Hey Mary, punk, prick pimps, I kinda like that. I think I'll use it in my next campaign."

—

On the drive in from the Hong Kong International Airport into the City's center, Nancy Cromwell sneezed into her kerchief and remarked, "We need to send Al Gore over here and have him clean this place up."

The thick layer of smog restricted visibility to about a quarter of a mile and the still air meant there was not going to be any relief for some time. Most of the other drivers and their passengers and the pedestrians wore surgical style masks not realizing it helped little except for spreading any virus they might be carrying to those nearby.

"Yeah, the United Nation's international regulations on carbon emissions haven't affected the Chinese much, unless they're hosting some international event like the Olympics," her husband Steve remarked.

"Well, the weather report calls for a stiff ocean breeze for this evening which should bring with it some relief, but also the aromas from the fish market," Ian chuckled and added, "Anyway, we only have to tolerate this for one night. Tomorrow night we'll be moving to the safe house in the hills," Ian said.

The taxi pulled into the circle of the 'Metropark Hotel' on Hennessey Road and parked. The trio exited and walked to the entrance while a red cap piled their luggage on a baggage cart and followed them into the hotel lobby.

"It's kind of weird being in the middle of China and staying at an English named hotel on an English named street," Nancy commented.

"Actually, Hong Kong is not really considered the middle of China. According to the treaty in 1997 when the Brits conceded rule to the Chinese People's Republic, Hong Kong would remain semi-independent from the home rule. English remains a co-official language and the Hong Kong District maintains an independent police force, but make no mistake, the end game of the Chinese Politico is to boot the Brits totally out one day," Ian explained.

Cover for their mission was being provided by the Superintendent of the White Cross Blood Transfusion Centre with the help and urging of Bernard Rusk. Ian paraded as a Hematologist and Steve and Nancy were his assistants. Ostensibly, they were here to instruct the staff on newly adopted screening methods for the detection of AIDS contamination in collected blood donations.

That evening, as they were making themselves comfortable in their new surroundings, Grant Wilson and Jesse Leone were paddling their two man raft up onto the sandy shore at the east bank of Bangkok Bay. They had launched the outdrive motored raft two hours earlier from the deck of a U.S. Navy Frigate anchored in the China Sea and they had cut the engine about a mile from shore in favor of rowing to maintain silence.

As they were dragging the raft up the beach, three local villagers emerged from the tree line and two of them latched onto the raft to assist and the third gave the much larger Grant a hug and said in broken English, "Sergeant Grant, it's so good to see you again."

"Hey Chaulkie, how the hell are you?" Grant beamed, picking up the man and swinging him around.

The man's given name was Chok Tau, and some years ago he and other village men had participated in a Navy Seal Black Operation to assassinate the local communist sympathizer War Lord who had been raiding local villages and robbing them of their crops and kidnapping some of their young women. Anyone who resisted him was slaughtered.

After unloading their gear and burying the raft with leaves and sand Grant and Jesse were escorted a short distance to the village of bamboo hutches with banana leaf roofs built on stilts a good four feet off the ground. They were greeted with open arms by the other villagers and a wild boar was roasting over any open campfire in their honor.

While feasting on the wild boar and other Thai delicacies, Jesse asked Tau, "So, since we did away with that War Lord, has life for you and your friends improved?"

"Somewhat," Tau replied and continued, "We no longer fear outside forces invading our villages, but the cor-cori-corptup the cor..."

"You mean the corruption?" Grant interrupted.

"Yes, the corruption still exists. As the City grows nearer to our village it tempts our young people. Last week one of my nieces and her friend ventured into Bangkok and we haven't seen them since. We went to the police and even the Provincial Magistrate, but I believe they have done nothing."

"What have you been doing about this?" Jesse asked.

"We have organized others with equal concerns and have demonstrated in front of the State House, but it does little good," Tau said.

"Maybe you should fight fire with fire," Grant suggested.

"What does that mean?" Tau asked tilting his head.

"That brings us to why we are here and have asked for your help, but let us enjoy this feast and we'll talk later," Jesse said.

CHAPTER FOUR

The City was beginning to wake up and the automated street lights were recognizing the dawn's arrival and blinking off as three SFPD Officers dressed is full SWAT outfits and gear approached the door to the 'Gentleman's Spa and Massage Parlor' located on the bottom floor of a three story structure on Bacon Street. Two of the Officers carried fully automatic AR16 rifles and the third toted a battering ram. Three other Officers, similarly dressed and armed stood at the rear door of the establishment in the back alley prepared to kick-off 'Operation Fun-Dee'.

Standing several yards behind the entry team with her 9mm semi-automatic sidearm raised and resting on her cheek was Ramona Vasquez. With a nod of her head, the man carrying the ram swung it forcefully forward and slammed it with precision against the door which flew open. He took a step back allowing his fellow Officers entry and then followed them in yelling, "San Francisco Police, we have a search warrant! Now, everyone show yourselves with your hand raised!"

Simultaneously, the three Officers at the rear door did the same thing. Behind a windowed counter inside the reception room stood a terrified, sleepy eyed young Asian woman with her arms raised.

Fifteen minutes later one of the Officers emerged from the front door and taking off his helmet he approached Inspector Vasquez and said, "All clear, Ma'am."

"Thank you Sergeant MacDonald," Vasquez replied as she holstered her weapon and entered the building.

Inside the reception area Officers were escorting young Asian women from a hallway entrance to the right of the counter window into the room. The women were skimpily clad and some looked as young as eleven or twelve years old. Behind the counter in a small office an Officer stood guard over two older Asian women and three younger males.

"It seems the three young punks were guards, one on each floor. They were all armed with Uzi's, so we have them on at least possession of an illegal firearm. We've got three Johns being held in the first room down the hall," MacDonald commented.

"Let's cuff all of them and get them in the bus transport. Issue each of these girls a blanket to cover themselves," Vasquez ordered.

"We might have a slight problem. One of the Johns claims to be a member of the Mayor's staff," MacDonald said

"I don't give a shit! Cuff him and make sure he's the first one off the bus when it gets to the gymnasium," Vasquez said.

Dinosa was supervising the work at the gymnasium. Cages borrowed from the San Francisco Zoo lined one corner of the room and cots were set up in rows in the opposite corner. Four portable cubicles with desks were set up at center court and an Assistant D.A., a SFPD Interrogator and an interpreter were assigned to each desk. Next to the far end of the room's entrance a make shift booking department had been set up complete with a photography booth, finger print identification area and DNA collection station.

She gathered all the people involved and said, "Okay, let's go over everybody's assignment so this doesn't look too much like a zoo. Sergeant Moon," she looked at John Moon, a second generation Korean American who worked in Public Affairs, "You and your men will consult with the arresting officer and separate each group into two categories as they file off the buses. You'll kindly escort the working girls to the holding area over there and assign each one a cot. The older Madams, pimps, thugs and Johns you will shackle together and treat as ordinary perps and process them through Booking and place them in a cage. Identify all of them with a check mark on their right arms with a non-indelible ink pen using a different color indicating from which establishment they were transported from."

Turning her attention to the four interrogation teams, she continued, "Marjorie and Michelle, I want your teams to interrogate the working girls using the questionnaire you've been given as an outline. Mark and Richard, you'll do the same with the Madams, pimps and Johns. I've selected you two women to the working girls, because I don't want them feeling any more intimidated than they already are. Remember these girls are victims, not criminals."

The bus from the 'Asian Spa and Massage Parlor' pulled up to the gymnasium's entrance and Sergeant MacDonald was the first to exit. He was met by Sergeant Moon and as the others exited they were marked on their arms with a blue pen and separated into two groups.

The first group escorted into the gym was the young working girls. They were led to the cots and each was assigned one. Most of them looked frightened and confused and Dinosa sighed, "Pathetic."

As the next group was ushered in, an older Asian woman shackled near the center of the line yelled in Thai at the young women, now sitting on cots, "You will keep your mouths shut or you will receive the ultimate sanction!"

Dinosa grabbed the arm of a nearby interpreter and asked, "What did she just say?"

After she was told, she yelled, "Sergeant Moon, muzzle that one! I want her first in line for booking," and then with a smile she added, "That one, I'll interview."

Dinosa followed the woman through the booking process and the woman stood defiantly in front of the camera when her muzzle was removed. After her front and profile pictures were taken the escorting Officer started to put the muzzle back on and Dinosa smiled and said, "That won't be necessary."

She collected the woman's paper work and grabbed the woman by her arm and led her to a curtained cubicle and entered. She sat the woman down on a stool next to a table and took the chair on the other side.

She leaned back in the chair and thumbed through the paper work and then chuckled and said, "I see you call yourself Mi Lik Yoo. That's cute, but with a face like yours I don't think you're getting rich sucking cocks."

The Asian woman sat mute defiantly staring at nothing as Dinosa continued to read through the reports.

"Do you need an interpreter?" Dinosa finally asked.

"I need a lawyer and I need to make my phone call," the woman responded in very good English.

The curtain parted and an Officer handed her another sheet of paper. Dinosa thanked him and perused the new report.

"Oh, I see you're from Hong Kong and your Passport and Visa information tells me you're here on a work visa. You arrived at San Francisco International Airport ten years ago and have made several trips back to your country of origin and your actual name is Michelle Lee. This says you work in the food service industry which, I'm going to presume, explains your alias.

"Now, let me tell you how this is going to work. You are a foreign national and you are being treated as a foreign terrorist and you are being charged with twenty-five counts of conspiracy to murder, illegal trafficking of under aged girls and narcotics, the illegal operation of a house of prostitution, interstate transportation of under aged girls for sexual purposes, and I'm sure before this is done I'll come up with a dozen more. When you are convicted you will be sentenced to death.

"As a foreign terrorist, you will be turned over to Home Land Security and you have no rights to an attorney. You will be transported from here to a Federal facility for interrogation and you won't be given the opportunity to talk to your people. It will take one call from me to make that happen. Now, does that appeal to you, or would you rather have a little chat with me?"

The woman remained stoic, but Dinosa did detect her legs were shaking slightly. Dinosa waited for a moment and then said, "Fine," picked up the telephone and began dialing.

"Wait," the woman said, "I have murdered no one."

Dinosa sat the telephone receiver down and reached into her valise and produced a stack of photographs and spread them on the desk before Lee and said bitterly, "These are pictures of chained young girls being flung over board from a ship located in our territorial waters. We have a video that shows twenty-five victims being hurled to their certain deaths."

Lee raised her hand to cover her mouth and moaned, "I had nothing to do with this. You cannot tie me to this."

"Apparently you don't understand the complicity and conspiracy laws of this country," Dinosa said and then lied, "We know some of these girls were tagged for your whore house. Our laws say that if you are involved with criminal activity that leads to murder, you are as culpable as the actual murderers. I'm sure you're aware that many of these girls have washed up on our shores and have outraged our citizens. You will get no sympathy from anyone and I will be hailed as a hero," Dinosa spat out.

"W-what do you need to know?" the now frightened woman asked.

Dinosa reached behind her and switched on a video camera mounted atop a tripod. She read the woman her rights and when the woman looked at her confused, Dinosa jutted her chin and asked menacingly, "Do you understand your rights and do you want to talk to me and answer my questions?"

"Oh, yes, yes," the woman replied.

Dinosa learned that Michele Lee worked for Billy Choo and managed the Asian Spa and Massage Parlor. The facility was leased under her name and Choo would collect the rent and ninety percent of the profits on a weekly basis. She was allowed to keep ten percent to pay herself and to cover overhead costs which included feeding and clothing the girls. Every few weeks Choo and several of his thugs would show up and drop off several new girls and take away several. She knew enough not to ask questions.

She did admit she believed most of the girls were under age and were not U.S. citizens nor was she ever shown work visas. She reminded Dinosa that she knew nothing and was not allowed to ask questions and she merely followed her boss' rules.

"Who provides them with drugs?" Dinosa asked.

"Billy Choo or one of his men would show up every afternoon to administer a shot of heroine, he says will keep them under control and passive," she replied meekly.

Marjorie parted the curtain and leaning in said, "Mary, sorry for the interruption, but I think you want to hear this."

"Stay right there," Dinosa said pointing a finger at Ms. Lee.

Walking together across the gymnasium floor, Marjorie said, "Two of the girls are Caucasian. They're fingerprints identify them as two missing cousins from Akron, Ohio. The girl in my cubicle is Janis Smith and her cousin is Sharon Smith. They went missing about a year ago when they were thirteen and fourteen years old. According to their parents they were walking to a game arcade about six blocks from one of their homes and never returned.

"The FBI has been informed and they've asked us to hold them until Special Agent Joan Richards arrives. She's in route from Reno."

They arrived at Marjorie's cubicle and a small, blond haired young girl sat shivering with a blanket wrapped around her on a chair in the corner. Mary grabbed Marjorie by her arm and directed her a few feet away.

"Holy shit, what does she have to say?" Mary asked disgustedly with her hand over her mouth.

"Not much, she's frightened to death," Marjorie replied.

Dinosa took a moment to think and then dialed Valerie Kane's office. She explained the situation and added, "Val, these girls have been through enough and I want to make this as easy and as comfortable for them as possible. They need immediate medical attention for their addiction and their going to need their parents. What do you suggest?"

"If you don't think they need emergency care, you transport them to Solomon Goldsmith's house. Do you know where he lives?" Kane said.

"Yes, on Cliff House Avenue. Ian and I have been there before, but what about health care, custodial transfer, the FBI and God only knows what else?" Dinosa said rolling her eyes up in despair and frustration.

"Don't worry about those things. I know a Judge who is very sympathetic to this sort of situation and Sol's home has already been designated as an approved SFPD and Family Services 'safe house'. I'll let the FBI and her parents know and I'll arrange for a Physician to meet you there. You just worry about getting the girls there," Kane responded.

After hanging up, Dinosa walked into the cubicle and crouched down in front of Janis Smith and gently laying her hand on her shoulder she said quietly, "Janis, I want you and your cousin to know you are safe now. We're going to take you to a nice home and you'll be reunited with your parents soon. You're going to have to remain strong for your younger cousin. Okay?"

The young girl raised her head and Mary detected a glimmer of suspicious hope on her face and then a tear fell from an eye as she nodded yes.

—

The seasonal monsoon rain fell like the beginning of Noah's biblical flood and visibility was poor as the pair dressed in dark khaki overalls and black knitted skull caps paddled their raft up to the port side of the 'Neap Tide' trawler. After tying off to the ship, Jesse glanced at his watch and then nodded at Grant.

They simultaneously tossed grappling hooks up and over the ship's side rail. The hooks landed with a clank and they prayed the sound was muffled by the torrential rain falling. They yanked and secured the hooks and then waited to see if any curious crew members would be attracted to the sound. A moment later Grant gave the thumbs up sign and after slinging their Mack Ten fully automatic weapons over their shoulders, the two scaled the side to the boat's gunnel and peered onto the deck. The deck was dimly lit by a single lamp and they noticed only one crew member with his back toward them and hunched down by the boarding gate. He wore a poncho to protect himself from the elements and was sipping from a bottle they hoped was an alcoholic beverage.

They hopped over the rail and as Grant unshouldered his weapon, Jesse produced an eight inch blade seal knife from its belt sheath. Like a stalking panther, Jesse quietly covered the distance between himself and the unsuspecting guard. Jesse wrapped his arm around the man's head and pulled it back into his chest and in one motion brought the razor sharp blade across the man's neck, severing his carotid artery on both sides and his wind pipe.

The man's initial scream turned to a gurgle and Jesse held him tight until the man's body went limp. Jesse released him and the dead body slumped to the deck. When he looked up he saw Chok Tau and two other men emerge from behind a freight container on the dock and approach the ship.

The three men joined Grant and Jesse on board and Grant, in a whisper asked, "How many other crewmen?"

"Four others plus the Skipper, he's a big fat ugly bastard and not too long ago he dragged one of the girls into his cabin over there," Tau said pointing at a door next to a ladder that led to the fly bridge at the ship's stern, and then continued, "The other four are in the crew's quarters through that door on the right."

"Where are they keeping the rest of the girls?" Jesse asked.

Tau pointed to a hatch cover on the foredeck and said, "There."

"Okay, you and your men wait here and when we give you the all clear you can open that hatch and escort the girls ashore," Jesse said and turning to Grant he said, "Let's go."

When they reached the cabins, each stood beside a door facing each other with their Mack Tens at the ready. Jesse nodded and they both slammed in the doors.

Jesse entered a dark cabin and finding the wall switch and flicking on the light he saw the naked rear end of a fat Asian man who was on top of a young naked girl on a cot in the corner of the room. The man was blinking, looking back at Jesse and angrily bellowed in Thai, 'Who the fuck are you!"

Jesse took two quick steps forward and slammed the butt of his weapon against the man's nose. He grabbed the man's leg and yanked him from the cot and his head banged hard off the deck. The large man rolled over and started to get up. Jesse gave him a straight kick to the jaw and the man went down and didn't move.

Grant entered a smoke filled room. Three men were sitting around a table near the door playing cards. On a lower bunk at the back of the room another man was humping on a whimpering young girl.

In Thai, Grant yelled, "Nobody move!"

In the other room, Jesse rolled the fat man on his belly and with zip ties, cuffed the man's hands behind his back. He looked at the terrified young girl who was holding a sheet to cover her trembling, naked body.

"It will be okay, honey. You're safe now," he said calmly.

He stepped out and gave Tau the all clear sign and then stuck his head inside the crew's cabin. Grant had the four men lined up facing the wall and was making the three clothed men disrobe. Jesse walked in and one by one cuffed the men's hands behind their backs and their ankles together with zip ties.

They asked the young girl to get dressed and then Jesse escorted them to where Tau was helping the other young girls out of the fish hold.

As one girl climbed out of the hold she screamed in Thai, "Uncle Chok, Uncle Chok! I knew you would come for me!"

She ran to Tau who lifted her off her feet and they embraced. "Oh Chi, your parents will be so pleased," he whispered in her ear, tears streaming down his cheeks.

Jesse turned around and observed two more young Thai men escorting a middle aged Caucasian couple on board. They were both shackled and the woman looked defiantly at Jesse, who said, "Mr. and Mrs. Johansson, so nice of you to join us."

Mrs. Johansson jutted her jaw and through clenched teeth snarled, "This is kidnapping and I'll see you rot in jail. I demand to be taken to the American Embassy, now!"

"But Mrs. Johansson, you'll be missing your free cruise for two aboard this luxury liner in the fish hold suite," Grant said sarcastically.

"You can't do this…" Mrs. Johansson protested before Grant interrupted and said seriously, "Oh yes we can and yes we are. You and your husband are going to enjoy the same accommodations you provided for so many innocent young girls."

He gagged the couple and led them down and into the reeking fish hold. Once inside, he pushed the two down on to grimy and soiled mattresses and then produced a brick of C-4 from his satchel along with a fuse attached to a black box detonator. He attached the device to the rear bulkhead and threw a switch that turned on a green light. He proceeded to place several other similar devices around the compartment, including one in clear view of the two people sitting on the mattresses and now shackled to the filthy commode.

He started to ascend the exit ladder, stopped near the top, turned and said, "Oh, so you know, when that green light on that little box in front of you turns red, you'll have about five seconds to make amends with the devil."

When he emerged from the hold he let the hatch drop with a loud clank and observed Jesse at the boarding gate talking to Tau.

"Once you've gotten the girls aboard the bus, take them to the address I gave you. It is a Catholic Sanctuary run by Sister Mary. She knows you're coming and will know what to do," Jesse said to his friend.

"How can we ever repay you?" Tau said, his voice breaking up.

"You already have, my friend," Jesse said and they hugged one another. When Tau turned to leave, Grant yelled after him in Thai, "Take care of those girls and God speed!"

Alone now on the deck Grant said, "Let's get to work."

Together they hefted their two man raft aboard and Grant, after looking in on and making sure their prisoners were still confined, made his way to the engine room. Jesse untied the mooring lines and tossed them on the dock and then climbed the ladder and entered the fly bridge. Before long the large fishing trawler inched away from the dock and out into the harbor. Half an hour later the engines went quiet and Grant emerged from the engine room. The ship now lay dead in the water in the middle of Bangkok Bay.

Jesse reached the bottom of the ladder and entered the Captain's cabin. The fat Captain sat naked in front of his bunk with his hand shackled behind him to the bed frame and his legs spread eagle with each ankle shackled with chains attached to opposite bed posts.

He sat a C-4 brick down on the deck between the man legs and close to his crotch, threw the switch, smiled and said, "Well buddy, I guess this is good-bye. By the way, I've set the timer on this one to go off about three seconds before the others. When that green light turns red, you have about two seconds. I wanted you to be the first one to meet your maker, no need to thank me."

He exited the cabin and met Grant leaving the crew's cabin. They lowered the raft over the side and then climbed down and boarded. They motored about five hundred yards from the 'Neap Tide' and Jesse put the outboard motor in idle. Grant held up the transmitter and depressed the red button. Two seconds later a bright ball of fire appeared on the 'Neap Tide's' deck, followed by multiple explosions that blew the center of the ship out of the water and broke it in two.

They braced themselves for the sound and concussion and when it hit them, Grant said calmly, "Adios, mother fuckers."

Five hours later they were helped aboard the U.S. Navy Frigate in the China Sea.

Yung Lan Road wound through the forest up into the hills and left the Hong Kong basin behind them as Ian drove the rented Land Rover with his passengers Steve and Nancy on board. Observing the on board GPS monitor, Steve said, "The driveway should be on our right just after this curve ahead."

Steve slowed the vehicle and after negotiating the curve made a right turn onto a single lane dirt and gravel road. He stopped the SUV and Nancy jumped out and wedged a motion detector device between the two branches of a Banyan tree, aimed it toward the driveway and switched it on.

Stepping back into the Land Rover and taking a deep breath she remarked, "Wow, the smell of the Magnolias is wonderful after inhaling that poison air down town."

The driveway made a sweeping turn and ended about two hundred feet further down the lane at the carport wedged between two small bungalows. Steve pulled into the carport and the three exited the vehicle and unloaded their baggage and gear. Once inside the bungalow on the right, Nancy looked around the living room and walked down the hall to inspect the bedrooms. Steve went directly to the kitchen and opened the fridge and smiled. He pulled out three bottles of Tsingtao beer and found an opener in a cabinet drawer.

When he reentered the living room he found Ian setting up the motion detector receiver on the coffee table and handed him a beer. He sat one of the other beers down on the table for Nancy and announced, "I'm going outside and look around."

After he left, Nancy entered the room, grabbed the beer and plopped down on an easy chair and said, "There're two bedrooms. The one on the left has a double bed and the one on the right has two twin beds. I claimed the double bed for us and there's a bathroom at the end of the hall."

"That's fine…" Ian started and was interrupted by a beep from the motion detector. He grabbed a pistol from the bag next to him, rushed to the window on the left of the door and motioned Nancy to cover the other window.

Pulling back the shade, he noticed Steve had taken cover behind a Banyan tree on the far side of the driveway and was crouched down with his weapon raised. A moment later a motor scooter emerged from the bend in the driveway and pulled up and parked behind the Land Rover. The rider got off the scooter and removed his helmet.

Ian said, "It's okay," and opening the door he greeted the new arrival, "Hey Gary, it's good to see you."

Steve followed Gary Brown into the bungalow and after introductions were made, Nancy said, "We've heard about you. Welcome back from the dead."

"Yeah, and Rusk has briefed me on all of you and I must say, I'm honored to be a part of your team, but Gary Brown is dead. I'm William Gray, a freelance travel log journalist and," he said looking at Ian, "it's important that you refer to me as William or Bill Gray."

While the others were contemplating the sacrifices and complications this total change of identity must incur, Gray reached in his satchel and produced that day's copy of the Hong Kong Royal Times newspaper and opened it to page three and spread it out on the kitchen counter. Everyone gathered around and pointing to an article under the headline; FISHING TRAWLER MYSTERIOUSLY BLOWS UP IN BANGKOK BAY, and underneath the sub-headline read; *Harbor Police Fear All Aboard are Lost,* Gray commented, "It looks like your friends succeeded in their mission."

Steve retrieved another beer from the fridge and after handing it to Gray, he raised his bottle and with a wide grin, said, "We don't like failure. Here's to Grant and Jesse."

The group moved to the living room and Steve plugged a thumb drive into the big screen television and turned it on. The image of a chubby Asian man with short cropped hair appeared on the monitor.

As Steve scrolled through the slide show presentation that showed pictures of the same man at various angles in different situations and events, he said, "This is our target here in Hong Kong, Chon Gai, President and CEO of a company called Asian Exports. I'm sure he's aware of what happened in San Francisco and yesterday in Bangkok, so he's going to be a little paranoid and his personal security will be on high alert.

"Our intelligence reports he's probably already in the process of arranging for a different method of transporting his sex trafficking trade to the States. He has recently met with a man named Baku Akmuhara from Somalia. Baku is a Somalian war lord who has realized the profits of sex trafficking and heads up that business in northern Africa.

"Believe it or not, sex trafficking has become an international syndication and is well organized and encompasses nearly every country of the world. It has become a multi-billion dollar enterprise. The syndicates act independently, trading girls to each other and transporting them mainly to the richer Arabian States, North and South America, China and anywhere they find people who are willing to pay for the use of their product.

"Rusk has organized what we can call an international task force to combat these despicable people. We are but one team he's organized to exterminate this virus. His group has similar teams in India, Kuwait, the United Kingdom, Russia, North Africa and the Netherlands.

"The idea is to pull their plug in a worldwide coordinated strike and flush these shits down the toilet. As it turns out, our team will have the hand on the flusher. Chon has called for a meeting of all the syndicate heads at his estate. We think that meeting will be held later this week."

Gray handed each of them a folder and continued, "Along with the pictures we've just seen, this folder contains satellite images and maps of the Chon estate. It also has updated security placements intelligence surrounding the estate and an information packet on each of the attendees. I suggest we independently study this material and then meet to lay out a plan of attack. By the way, Jesse Leone and Grant Wilson will be here in the morning."

—

CHAPTER FIVE

The young Physician closed the bedroom door gently behind her and walked down the hallway and met an anxious Dinosa and Sol Goldsmith in the living room. Seeing the worried expressions on their faces, she said, "I think they'll be okay. Janis has a mild yeast infection and both girls have bruising on their arms and legs," and then with disgusted sarcasm she added, "It seems their keepers weren't very gentle. I've given them both a sedative and prescribed an antibiotic for Janis. They appear to be well nourished and otherwise healthy. I guess these bastards figured unhealthy merchandise wasn't good for business. They also have a mild heroin addiction, but shouldn't suffer too badly from withdrawal.

"Nurse Karnowski, the lady from Family Services, is with them and she knows what she's doing. What they need now is love and compassion and reassurance that their nightmare is over and is not their fault. They both asked when they'd see their parents and all I could say was soon."

Looking at Dinosa, she said, "Maybe you can go in and reassure them. I have to get back to the hospital, but if you need anything, this is my card. Call me anytime."

She handed each of them her card and left the residence. Mary walked down the hall and tapped lightly before opening the door. Nurse Karnowski was sitting on a chair next to a queen sized bed. The two young girls were on top of the bed dressed in robes and Sharon appeared to be asleep with her head cradled and resting on her cousin's shoulder.

Dinosa walked over and holding Janis' free hand whispered, "Your parents will be here in about three hours. Can I get you anything?"

"No thank you," Janis replied through sleepy and grateful eyes.

"You've been a very brave girl and I know your parents will be proud of you. When your mother was contacted she said her prayers had been answered. Try to get some rest so you'll be ready for the big reunion," Dinosa whispered.

She patted Nurse Karnowski on the shoulder as she exited the room and rejoined Goldsmith in the living room.

"You know Sol," she sighed, "we've seen a lot over the last few years, but this has to be the most pathetic. Just tell me Bernie Rusk, Ian and your group are going to put an end to this awful business."

"Only the Almighty can answer that for you, but you can rest assured, we'll all be giving it our best effort to help Him," Goldsmith replied.

They were interrupted by the sound of the front doorbell. Sol answered the door and observed a cute, pixie like young woman dressed in a navy blue, straight cut suit, wearing horn rimmed glasses with a large briefcase strapped over her shoulder and hanging like an anchor off her left thigh.

"Mr. Solomon Goldberg, I'm FBI Special Agent Joan Richards," she informed him formally and business like. She continued in a like manner, "District Attorney Investigator Mary Dinosa, I believe is expecting me."

"Please come in. May I take your bag?" Goldsmith asked, stifling a chuckle.

Richards followed him across the foyer and into the living room and he introduced her to Dinosa.

Goldsmith said, "Please have a seat and make yourself comfortable. I'll fetch us some tea."

He left the room and Richards remained standing and addressing Dinosa said, "I understand the Smith cousins are here. It's imperative I question them immediately."

"Yeah, well that ain't gonna happen, at least not immediately," Dinosa snapped.

"Listen," Richards started with her voice raised, "I'm leading a Federal investigation and I demand that you take me to them now or you will be subject to arrest for interfering with said investigation!"

"No, you listen!" Dinosa responded, raising her voice above Richards'. She was about to voice her objections to whom she believed was another self-righteous, tight-assed, straight-laced Fed. She paused remembering the advice given to her by Valerie Kane dealing with tact.

Smiling she continued in a calm voice, "I think we started off on the wrong foot. Please sit down and let me explain. These young girls, as I'm sure you can appreciate, have been to hell and back. They're frightened and confused. We brought them here because it was a safe and comfortable environment. A Physician just left and she gave them both a mild sedative. A Registered Nurse from Family Services is with them now in a back bedroom and they're sleeping right now. There will be plenty of time to interview them later.

"Now, if you insist on questioning them now, I will arrest them and charge them with prostitution. Under the laws of California they are considered minors and cannot be questioned without the presence of a parent. I don't think either one of us wants that. So, why don't you take a seat and the two of us cut the official bull shit and just talk woman to woman."

Richards plopped her brief case on the floor and sat down on an easy chair and sighed, "You're right. I apologize for the, as you put it, official bull shit. It's just that I've been on this task force for over a year and I'm exhausted. I've followed these two girls all over the country and always been a stop behind them."

"Task force," Dinosa questioned, "what kind of a task force?"

"After the Smith cousins were kidnapped and we discovered they were sold into the sex slave market, my boss convinced the Justice Department that this was a growing national crime after our initial investigation uncovered a syndicated business that traded and sold these girls across State borders and it also included international trade.

We needed to devote a special federal task force to investigate these people and bring them to justice. Fortunately the Attorney General agreed," Richards explained.

"Why haven't we been informed of this task force?" Dinosa asked.

"Because we didn't want it leaked to these corrupt assholes until we're ready," Richards replied.

Dinosa liked her choice of words and thought, maybe this gal isn't so bad after all.

She continued, "I'm not privy to all aspects of our internal investigation, but I believe we're close to serving arrest warrants for upwards of two hundred people nation-wide on Rico charges. I know here in the states we've identified the man at the top. His name is Jamal Franks, and believe it or not, he's a City Alderman from Detroit."

"What have you learned about their activities here in San Francisco?" Dinosa asked.

While the two exchanged and compared notes on their overlapping investigations, Goldsmith entered the room and sat a tea serving tray on the table and said, "Enjoy, I'll leave you two alone," and discreetly departed.

Dinosa learned after the Smith cousin's abduction, Richards followed their trail to a sleazy motel on the outskirts of Indianapolis where they were sold to a pimp who catered to drivers parked over night at the truck stop across the interstate highway. They were then taken to Detroit and made to ply their trade on the streets of the slum ridden city. About three months later they were moved to Biloxi, Mississippi where their bodies were again sold on the streets.

After that stop, Richard lost track of the girls for several months until she learned they had resurfaced in Denver, Colorado. She believed she missed them when she arrived in Denver by no more than two days. From there, a tip took her to Reno, Nevada.

At each location, she uncovered and implicated at least one pimp and sometimes even his boss. She reported all of this to her superiors and was told because of her work and others, the Agency had convinced the Attorney General to authorize the task force and issue the arrest warrants.

"That and meeting the girl's parents kept me going," Richards concluded.

Dinosa tilted her head, looked oddly at Richards and asked, "Do you know a man named Bernard Rusk?"

"His name sounds familiar. Why do you ask?"

"He's a Deputy Director at the CIA and heads up their International Crime Division, among other things," Dinosa replied with a wry smile punctuating the end of her statement.

She continued, "I know he's investigating the international sex trade enterprises and I have an idea that he's behind holding up the serving of your arrest warrants. He's a very influential character and I believe his intention is to bring down the entire world-wide network. Like your agency, he doesn't want to show his hand to these assholes."

Richards placed her chin on her palms, rubbed her eyes and said, "You know Mary, sometimes working for the FBI I get frustrated, questioning the orders I'm given and the decision making of my superiors. In the end I just do the best I can based on faith and sometimes that gets a little wobbly. Thanks for restoring some of that."

"Joan, you look exhausted. Why don't you lie down on that couch and catch a nap? You'll need to be wide awake when we interview the Smith girls. I'll get a comforter for you," Mary suggested.

—

Bernard Rusk sat at his desk in the make shift office at the U.S. Naval Base, Guantanamo Bay, Cuba. He had just come from an interrogation of a Gitmo detainee who claimed to have new information that would lead to the top of the African black market diamond smuggling cartel. It turned out the man had nothing to add to the international investigation, but Rusk felt obliged to question the man at the request of his friends at Interpol.

He unsealed the CIA envelope labeled 'Top Secret', delivered while he was interrogating the detainee. It was Grub's report. As he scanned the report he again marveled at the talent this man had. His computer skills were unmatched by anyone he had ever come across in his eighty-one years. He figured Grub could not only find a needle in a hay stack, but he could tell you where it was manufactured, how many garments it had sewn, socks it had darned and most importantly, who profited from its' labor and where the money was and have no knowledge of where physically the hay stack was located.

Grub's report consisted of forty-eight pages and the final page was a removable fold out that after Rusk removed and unfolded it, the page covered over half the surface of his desk. Two pyramid columns branched from the top of the page with lines connected to blocks underneath that widened as it descended to their respective bases. With lines and arrows connecting boxes and interlinking some of them to several others, it looked more complicated and busier than an aerial view of a Los Angles major interstate exchange or an international interconnecting flight patterns with their final destinations being the North Pole.

Rusk focused on the names that headed each pyramid. At the top of the left column was a block titled 'the Huang Tong' and underneath the name 'Joey Wang' and in parenthesis 'see appendix one'. At the top of right column the block read 'the Black Brotherhood' and underneath the name 'Jamal Franks' and in parenthesis 'see appendix two'. A red line connected the two boxes.

He raised his eye brows and tilted his head and mumbled an audible, "Hum." He knew about the national syndicate of Jamal Franks and the Black Brotherhood and even knew that the organization was funneling funds to a militant faction of the Muslim Brotherhood in Syria to wage their holy war. He often wondered how this religion, a religion that relegated women to covering their entire bodies and demanded total purity and subjugation, could reconcile taking funds from the profits of men who enslaved and prostituted innocent young women. Not only a contradiction, but a major hypocrisy he concluded. What really raised his curiosity was the Huang Tong. He believed this group was under the umbrella of Jamal Franks' group, not an equal.

He thumbed back in the report to appendix one that concluded the Tong had received an estimated one billion dollars from the illegal sex slave trading in the United States and the majority of those profits were deposited in a Cayman Island bogus corporate account and redistributed to various accounts in Asia and North Africa. The final paragraph noted that account transfers between the Cayman Island account and a similar account set up by the Black Brotherhood in a Dubai account had ceased about six month ago and he speculated a power struggle had begun between the two groups.

Rusk raised his head and with a wry smile mumbled out loud again, "Interesting."

Turning back to the first page, he buried himself into reading the entire report. An hour later, after reading the complete report, he picked up the phone and dialed a number.

"Hey George, its Bernie, we need to talk. Would you get a hold of Sol and Sean and let's meet at your place tomorrow morning? And see if Ms. Dinosa can join us."

CHAPTER SIX

The maroon Subaru Outback pulled up and parked in front of the bungalows and Jesse and Grant exited the vehicle. Ian O'Farrell was the first to greet them and hailed, "Job well done!"

After hugs and handshakes all around, Jesse said, "We come bearing gifts. We received orders to pick up a package at British Airways Freight when we landed. It's in the rear."

Grant opened the rear hatch which exposed a wooden crate measuring about two feet by three feet by four feet.

"Thank you Mister Rusk. You've delivered once again," Gary Brown exclaimed and added, "Come on, let's get this inside."

Once inside, Brown pried the lid off the crate and whistled, "Ladies and gentlemen, allow me to introduce you to the latest weapon in combating terrorism, the MXT 135 Rifle."

He reached in and produced one of the two rifles from its formed foam contoured location. Handing it to Grant he asked, "What do you think this is?"

To his surprise, Grant answered, "I know exactly what this is. Not that I've had personal interaction with it, but I've been reading about it. It fires a 35 mm round. The weapon's gun sight uses a laser range finder to determine the exact distance to a target or obstruction, after which the user can add or subtract by depressing this button above the trigger guard up to ten meters. That will enable the bullet to clear the barrier and explode above or beside the target. The 35 mm round contains a chip that receives a signal from the gun sight and detonates at the preprogrammed distance with the force and destructive power of a hand grenade. The weapon is semi-automatic with a three round capacity."

"Excellent, Sergeant Wilson, can you imagine the lives this weapon will save?" Brown said reaching down to lift the layer of foam rubber in the crate, exposing a dozen rounds for the MXT 135 Rifle. They appeared to be exploded views of a metal jacketed forty-four magnum bullet, approximately two inches in diameter and about four inches long.

"Hopefully our own," Jesse responded giving the sign of the cross.

"Okay, let's get down to the business at hand," Ian said leading the team to the kitchen table.

"This is a satellite map of the Chon Gai estate. Our intelligence tells us this is where most of the world's sex trade Pooh-Bahs will be meeting tomorrow and represents our best opportunity to eliminate them. The estate is located only three miles from here, farther up the canyon."

The Chon estate was located about one hundred yards off of Lung Yan Road at the end of a paved driveway. It was a sprawling connected u-shaped two story dwelling that surrounded a huge kidney shaped swimming pool on three sides. A large open cabana occupied the other side of the pool to the east. A ten foot concrete wall surrounded the estate and a foot path followed the wall's exterior. The jungle and debris had been cleared for about twenty yards around the path's perimeter.

"Now, the acquisition of these weapons will change our plans and somewhat make it easier. The three points of attack will remain the same, assuming it is within this weapon's range," Ian said looking at Brown for confirmation.

"No problem, the effective range is three hundred meters," Brown replied.

O'Farrell continued, "Our intel reports Chon is extremely security conscious and he conducts his important meetings under the cabana. It's surrounded with an anti-listening system and he feels safe there.

"So, we'll divide into three, two man teams. Gary and I will be team Alpha, Steve and Grant team Bravo, and Nancy and Jesse team Charlie. We'll have real time satellite surveillance on our I-Pads and will be able to adjust our fire accordingly.

"We reconned the site yesterday afternoon. We'll park the SUV here," Ian said pointing to a spot on the map of an overgrown unused path off of Lung Yan Road around a blind bend in the road about two hundred yards from the Chon estate.

He continued, "The vehicle will be hidden from the road. Beta Team will deploy to this spot. Steve scouted it yesterday and Charlie team will deploy to this spot with Nancy leading the way. Alpha team will travel out of sight to this spot," he pointed to a location in the tree line in front of the estate.

The attack sights for Beta and Charlie teams were separated about fifty yards apart in the tree and jungle line at the east side of the estate and only obstructed by the wall from the pool side cabana.

"Yesterday, we observed four sentries patrolling the path. Tomorrow will be different with all off the big shots arrivals. We anticipate a little tighter security. We'll all be hooded and equipped with earwigs and lapel microphones for communication. When I've determined the time is right, I'll give the three second countdown. After that there will be no turning back. At zero hour precisely, the two teams will fire their MXT 135 rifles aimed and programmed to converge directly above the cabana. Immediately adjust your aim to about ten yards left and right of the cabana and fire again.

"Wait for the smoke to clear and consult your I-Pads. If you decide another shot is unnecessary, pick up your AR16s and assist your partner who will already be eliminating the perimeter guards. It's important that all of the guards be immobilized to protect our withdrawal. Is that clear?" O'Farrell asked.

After receiving everyone's affirmative nods, he continued, "When the shit starts, Brown and I will eliminate the chauffeurs and disable all of the vehicles and proceed to the house. We'll clear the house and contain any servants to one room and mop up any stragglers.

"You guys remain at your stations as our back-up and when I give the word we will all withdraw to the SUV, return to the bungalows and prepare for our get out of Dodge plans. I'm buying the first round at Zack's Bar and Grill in Sausalito."

Bernard Rusk sat in the den of the Armstrong residence in Los Altos California, surrounded by members of the Justice Foundation along with Mary Dinosa and addressed the group, "Good to see you all," he began, "and congratulations on your team's success in Bangkok. Coupled with a similar outcome of their operation in Hong Kong should bring an end to one of the world's largest players in the sex trade industry. You should know that like operations are being conducted in North Africa, the Middle East, Europe and Russia and we're not just hitting the supply side, but the demand side also. It's one thing for men to hire adult escorts and women who sell their sexual favors, it's quite another thing for men who would abuse and include innocent children to fulfill their perverted desires.

"As we bust the king pins and pimps, we're gathering information on their clients and distributing it to local and state law enforcement. They will face a day of reckoning soon."

He glanced at Dinosa to solicit a response. She stood and spoke, "Yes, I just met with the FBI task force investigating the illegal sex trade in this country and I must say I was surprised at the information they have gathered and shared with us."

She clicked a remote control and a corporate leadership chart appeared on the large screen television mounted on the far wall. With a laser pointer she aimed it at the top of the chart titled the 'Huang Tong' and to the name 'Joey Wang'.

"This is the son of a bitch at the top of one of two syndicates in the country responsible for the import and national distribution of minors. We're working with the feds to tie him directly to the murders of the young girls that have washed up on our shores."

She aimed the pointer at the name connected just below Wang at 'Billy Choo (Wah Ching Gang)' and continued, "This is Mr. Wang's captain and leader of the Wah Ching Gang in Chinatown. This little punk is responsible for leading a group of gang bangers and pimps that are involved in distributing illegal drugs, arms and little girls. When the investigation is completed, every name on this chart and some that are not will be indicted on Rico and murder charges."

Gathering up her paper work and stuffing it in her shoulder bag, Dinosa said, "Well guys, as usual it's been a hoot, but I've got to get going."

After she departed, Rusk cleared his throat and said, "What I'm about to tell you, I thought, should be best said outside the presence of Ms. Dinosa since it could be considered outside the normal bounds of law enforcement."

A diagonal line from Joey Wang's name led to a box containing the name 'Asian Imports, Ltd.' above the names Ronald and Roselyn Bingham. Pointing the laser at this box, Rusk commented, "These are the people connected with their Bangkok and Hong Kong sister syndicate called 'Asian Exports, Ltd.' led by a man named Chon Gai. We've learned they are, along with most of the world's sex trade leaders, meeting at the Gai estate tomorrow. That is the target for your team and by this time tomorrow they should be on their way home and leave with the world sex slave market in turmoil."

"We have also uncovered two major players responsible for importing and distributing young girls in this country's sex trade. Besides the Huang Tong, the other big player is a group from Chicago headed by Alderman Jamal Franks from Detroit. Up until now, the two syndicates have cooperated with one another often trading product. That is about to change.

"Doctor Daniel Tanaka has traced most of these two entities profits to off shore bank accounts. He has hacked these accounts and has just transferred their balances to two other accounts. Grub, bless his heart, has left a footprint that can be surreptitiously traced back to their opposite parts. In other words, one group will believe the other group has drained and stolen their assets.

"The war has already started. Two of Franks' pimps have been shot down in Chicago and New York City and a Huang Tong cat house in Winnemucca, Nevada was raided and the hookers kidnapped. Don't ask me how he's done it, but Grub has arranged a peace talk meeting between the two groups. In five days the pow-wow will be held in the Mohave Desert. We'll make sure it's not a happy reunion.

"I think you'll all agree, justice is better served when it is self-inflicted."

Mary Dinosa straightened her suit jacket, shook and fluffed her hair, attempted to compose herself, looked at her wrist watch and mumbled, "shit," before she opened the door and walked into the conference room on the fourth floor of the Federal Building.

"Sorry everybody," she lied, "I got hung up at the security check downstairs."

Valerie Kane, sitting with four other people at a round table, simply looked sadly at her and shook her head. Dinosa recognized three of the four other people. One of them was FBI Special Investigator Joan Richards another was the DOJ Deputy Attorney General for the thirteenth district, Thomas Coburn, and the third was SFPD Chief Harold Hamm. She was introduced to Special Agent Bradley Stevens, in charge of the federal task force investigating the illegal sex trade in the United States.

"Thank you for joining us, Investigator Dinosa," Coburn said, "Now, let's get started. The reason I called for this meeting is to request the District Attorney's office and the SFPD to cooperate with our investigation and our federal prosecution cases. I'm sure that we can all agree that the Department of Justice has the best resources to bring these animals to justice."

Thomas Coburn was Valerie Kane's replacement at DOJ when she resigned to run for District Attorney and Kane respected his talent and dedication. She also realized he was right that the DOJ had far more resources than her financially strapped department.

"I have no problem with that," Kane started and continued, "There is no reason for duplicating each other's efforts. My hope is, all of these cases which we will be turning over to you will be charged under the ongoing criminal activity statutes and all of these people will be charged with the murders of the twenty-five women that were dumped in the ocean off our shores and some of whom washed up on our beaches."

"You have my word they will be. The bad news is, the ship's captain and crew were mysteriously assassinated in Thailand a few days ago. The good news is, our State Department won't have to waste a lot of time and resources trying to get them extradited," Stevens remarked.

Dinosa glanced at Kane with a knowing smile.

The group spent the next few hours comparing notes and developing strategies. Bradley Stevens briefed the group about the ongoing national investigation and the chain of command for the Huang Tong and the Jamal Franks' syndicate.

"I must apologize for not bringing your jurisdiction in on our plans and investigation, but we felt until we were ready to move, we couldn't risk the word getting out to forewarn these creeps. When we are prepared to act, we will inform you and work with local police agencies to bring this enterprise to an end in every major city in the nation. It will be the largest operation of this kind in this nation's history. I'm talking about literally thousands of arrests. You people, and I mean no offense, just got a little ahead of us. I must say you have provided us a blue print for our future operations. You did a hell of a job."

"So, I'm assuming this country-wide bust will be a coordinated, simultaneous effort. Can you tell us when it will happen?" Kane asked.

"Honestly, we're a little frustrated. We've got all our ducks in row and I'm just waiting for the okay from my boss. He says he can't tell me the reason for the delay, but I suspect it has to do with something going on similar to the mysterious assassinations in Thailand," Stevens replied.

Again, Dinosa glanced at Kane and batted her eyes and then asked, "How about our neighbors to the north and south?"

"We've shared our intelligence with the RCMP and they've conducted their own internal investigation and have agreed to wait for our go ahead. We've made the decision we can't take the risk of sharing our information with the Mexican government. After our operation is completed, we will pass along what information we have to the proper Mexican authority. Our State Department will apply pressure on them, but I think we all know what results that will bring. For now, we'll just have step up our efforts and try to intercept them at the border and points of entry," Stevens said.

Together and alone in the elevator after the meeting broke up, Kane turned to Dinosa and said, "Okay, what were all the smirky smiles and eye spasms all about?"

"All I know is, the same morning I met with Bernie Rusk and after he met with the Justice Foundation, Ian informed me he would be away for a while. A few days later the ship, captain, and crew were blown to kingdom come in Thailand. Ian still isn't home and Stevens figures the reason for delaying his plans is probably due to a similar overseas operation. You add it up," Dinosa quipped.

"Where is Ian now?"

"I don't have the slightest idea."

Jesse gave Steve and Grant the thumbs up sign as he and Nancy parted ways with Bravo team and made their way through Banyan and Eucalyptus trees and the underbrush to their designated attack point. Jesse found a low hanging Banyan tree branch and laid his MXT 235 rifle across the crotch where the limb and trunk met. He had a clear line of sight to the estate's ten foot concrete wall and the dozen sentries spaced evenly about ten yards apart along the west wall. The guards were all armed with what appeared to be Chinese made SKS fully automatic rifles. Nancy pulled out an I-Pod from her fatigue blouse and turned on the real time satellite image showing the estate.

She counted ten guards along the north wall and a like number along the south wall. Another three guards were inside the compound and surrounded the cabana.

She shared the screen with Jesse which now showed about a dozen people walking together next to the pool toward the cabana inside the compound. They disappeared under the cabana's roof. Jesse peered through his scope and range finder and adjusted the time delay for his rounds to detonate and explode directly above the cabana.

"Beta team positioned and ready," cackled over everyone's ear wigs.

In turn, Jesse reported, "Charlie team positioned and ready."

"Await my command," Ian said.

He and Gary Brown were making their way in the tree line on either side of the driveway to the estate's parking lot. Eight cars were parked in a line just in front of the elaborate entrance to the residence. The drivers were all gathered and sitting around an umbrella table in the front court yard chatting and smoking cigarettes.

Crouching and staying out of view from the drivers, Ian and Brown approached the line of cars from either side. Ian pulled his knitted ski mask down to conceal his identity and Brown did the same. They began attaching magnetic remote controlled IEDs to the under carriage of each vehicle until they met in the center.

They nodded at each other and Ian said into his microphone, "Commence firing on three, two, one."

A moment later two explosions could be heard coming from the rear of the estate. The startled drivers all jumped up, some reaching for weapons concealed under their jackets and other frozen in fear and panic.

From cover of the cars, Ian and Brown began spraying the table area with their AR16s. The surprised drivers never got the chance to return fire. In a matter of seconds they all lay dead or dying within several yards of the table. Small arms fire could be heard coming from the rear of the compound.

Ian retrieved his I-Pod as Brown surveyed the bodies and assured they were all dead by shooting them in the head with his 45 caliber sidearm. Looking at the I-Pod image, Ian could see the cabana was destroyed and bodies laid strewn about the yard. A man and a woman were hobbling alongside the pool and stumbling toward the residence.

Ian ordered, "Beta team, adjust for thirty meters past the wall and fire."

A moment later Ian watched on his screen as the round exploded almost directly above the struggling couple. When the smoke cleared, the two lay motionless beside the pool.

"Beta, Charlie, hold you're positions," Ian commanded and nodding at Brown, said, "Let's go!"

With a burst from his AR16, Brown shattered the lock on the outer cast iron gate and another burst knocked open the residence's entrance door on the far side of the porch foyer.

Brown was the first to enter and speaking Chinese, he bellowed, "If you are a house servant, show yourselves now and you will be spared! If you don't show yourselves with your hands over your head in five seconds you will be shot!"

Two young Asian women dressed in maid outfits emerged from the upstairs and stood at the top of a spiral staircase, both trembling with their hands above their heads. Another Asian young man appeared from an adjoining room in a similar fashion and another Asian man dressed in kitchen whites stumbled blindly, with his hands covering his bloody face, down a hall that led to the kitchen.

Speaking again in Chinese, Brown ordered, "All of you come over here."

Ian slung his rifle over his shoulder and led the wounded man and the other servants to a room off of the main entrance. He then stood guard at the door as Brown interrogated the group.

"We are not here to cause you any harm. It is your boss and his associates we are interested in and you probably know why. Now, are there any other guards or bad men in the house?" he questioned.

They each nodded negatively except for the wounded man in whites who whimpered, "The chef is still in the kitchen, but he is not a bad guy. His name is Jean Le Clerk."

Retrieving a first aid kit from his knapsack and handing it to one of the maids he said, "Please, do what you can for this man. Professional help will be here soon. I want all of you to stay in this room and I give you my word you will be safe."

Brown closed the door behind him as he left the room. As Ian started up the stairs taking them two at a time he yelled back, "I'll clear the upstairs and you do the same down here."

Brown proceeded to check several other rooms off the large entrance area and finding them unoccupied, he proceeded down the hall from where the kitchen servant had come. Several doors from the hallway led to bedrooms and another to an office. At the end of the hall, saloon style swinging doors led to the kitchen. He swung the doors open and stepped into the room with his rifle at the ready.

"Jean Le Clerk, show yourself and you will not be harmed!" he yelled.

A moment later from his crouched position behind an island counter, a tall lanky man dressed in kitchen whites donning a chef hat stood up with a raised meat clever and said in English with a heavy French accent, "What is it you want?"

The scene seemed comical to Brown and he snickered and said calmly, "Certainly not you. Now, drop the cleaver and come with me."

The Frenchman did as he was told and Brown led him back through the house and left him with the others. Coming down the stairs, Ian said, "The upstairs is clear."

"So is it down here," Brown replied.

They proceeded to the back yard and then separated and walked on either side of the pool toward the cabana. When Ian came upon the bodies of the previously fleeing couple, he first rolled over the man who was Caucasian. He was obviously dead. He retrieved a plastic bottle labeled 'DNA Swab Kit' from his satchel. He extracted the Q-tip from the bottle and swabbed the inside of the man's mouth. He did the same to the Asian woman who lay several yards from the man.

Ian and Brown traveled from body to body, first confirming they were dead and then performing the swabs. As Brown approached the last body and started to bend over him, the man suddenly rolled over and before Brown could react fired a round from a hand gun. Brown instinctively dove on top of the man, grabbing his pistol hand. Another shot rang out and blood from a head wound splattered on Brown's face as the man's body went limp.

Brown rolled off the man and looked over at Ian who was standing about twenty feet away, his rifle still aimed at the now dead man. He started to stand up when he realized he couldn't.

"Ah shit, I've been hit," he groaned, looking down at his side and the blood soaked hole in his fatigue jacket.

Ian rushed over and helping him to his feet said, "Come on, we gotta get out of here."

As he dragged Brown across the yard he said to the others, "Both teams proceed to the extraction point. Don't wait for us. We'll meet you at the Bungalows."

The two made it through the house and to the parking lot. Ian sat Brown down on the steps and ran to the line of cars. The first one he checked was a Cadillac Limousine and had the keys in the ignition. He removed the earlier placed IED, got in the car and started it up and spun gravel as he raced the car back to the stairs. He dragged Brown and laid him down in the rear seat and then sped out of the lot and down the driveway. At a safe distance he depressed a button on a remote control and heard a series of explosions coming from behind them as they turned onto the road at the end of the driveway.

They were about a mile down Lung Yan Road when they passed two Hong Kong police cruisers followed by an ambulance coming up the hill, lights flashing and sirens blaring.

"How are you doing?" Ian asked.

"I might live," Brown replied with a groan.

Beta and Charlie teams made their way back to the SUV and approached it with care. Finding the area clear they quickly stowed their gear in the back of the vehicle and jumped in. When they turned onto Lung Yan Road they met two troop carriers coming from the opposite direction. All eyes watched as the trailing vehicle pulled over to the roads shoulder and attempted to make a U-turn.

"Ah shit!" Grant moaned.

The SUV followed a curve in the road and the troop carrier disappeared from sight just as they saw it complete the U-turn and accelerate in pursuit. Around the next turn the SUV entered a deep ravine carved out of the hill side rock. As the vehicle exited the ravine, Jesse yelled at Steve, "Pull over and stop!"

Almost before the SUV came to a complete halt, Jesse was out of the passenger side door and ran to the rear of the vehicle and retrieved his MXT 135 rifle. Taking aim and adjusting the range finder detonator he fired. The round detonated as it came in contact with the ravine's wall about twenty yards up from the road. The explosion dislodged several large boulders and smaller debris that tumbled down the steep slope and settled on the road.

Satisfied the road would be impassible, Jesse returned to the SUV and hopping in snickered, "That should slow them down a bit."

When they reached the bungalows, they observed Ian dragging Brown into the nearest cabin. When they entered the front room, Brown was lying on the couch and Ian was bent over him unbuttoning Brown's shirt. Nancy rushed to the rear of the house and retrieved a first aid kit from the bathroom. Returning, she nudged Ian out of the way and knelt down beside the now shirtless Brown.

"It looks like a pretty clean through and through," Ian commented.

"Well, based on his color it looks like it's probably only nicked his liver and didn't hit any major arteries," Nancy said.

Brown lifted his head and groaned, "It's just a flesh wound."

"Oh shut up and be still," Nancy retorted as she applied gauze and started cleaning the wound with alcohol.

She covered the entrance and exit wounds with disinfected patches and then with the help of Ian, rolled Brown over and wrapped his midsection with gauze.

"He's going to need real medical attention soon," she exclaimed with a grimace.

Scratching the top of his head, Ian said, "Okay, you guys take the SUV to the boat. I'll take Brown in the Limo to the Red Cross Blood Depository. They have doctors there and can take care of him. If I'm not there by midnight, proceed with the extraction plan without me."

"That's bull shit," Brown protested. "You guys get the hell out of here. I can take care of myself."

"Yeah, and fuck you Gary. We leave no one behind," Ian replied.

It was 11:35 p.m. when the teams spotted the headlights come over the horizon and start down the winding road that ended at the coastal cove and their location.

"Start the engines, Ling," Steve said to the diminutive Asian man sitting in the pilot seat of the thirty-six foot cigarette boat, as the team spread out into the cover of the brush on the shoreline.

"Relax guys, it's only me," cackled in each of their ear wigs. They all exhaled a sigh of relief.

When the limo pulled up to the shanty beside the dock, Jesse was there to meet Ian and handed him a helmet.

"How's Gary?" he inquired.

"The doctor says he'll be okay. It'll be a few days before he can travel, but as far as we could tell, his cover hasn't been blown and William Gray should be good to go," Ian replied.

After they boarded the boat, Ian reiterated the story to the rest of the crew and strapped in after Ling said over the helmet intercom, "Hold 'em if you got 'em."

The bow lifted slightly and then settled down as the cigarette boat shot out of the cove and into open waters. They would make the Taiwan shore and Taichung City before sunrise and would board a commercial airline and be home within twenty-four hours.

CHAPTER SEVEN

Valerie Kane stood at the podium in front of the microphones and cameras in the media packed City Hall auditorium. She began, "I'm going to read a prepared statement and then I'll do my best to answer a few questions."

She cleared her throat and continued, "As you all know, four days ago in a cooperative and coordinated effort by this department and the San Francisco Police Department, we conducted numerous raids on known massage parlors, adult entertainment clubs, known houses of prostitution and several private residences and executed arrests warrants on their occupants.

"These raids were conducted in response to the drowning of twenty-five young girls who were murdered off our shores, some of whom washed up on our beaches one week ago. I cannot comment on particulars of the arrests as this is an ongoing investigation, but I can tell you that the citizens of our City, the Mayor's Office, the Police Department and the District Attorney's Office will not tolerate the illegal sex slave trade to find sanctuary in our City.

"Are there any questions?"

One voice drowned out the anxious reporters vying for attention, "Some people say, you're campaign is purposely targeting men who frequent these establishments who simply go there for rest and relaxation. Is there any truth to this?" Reginald 'Scoop' Jackson, a gossip columnist for the San Francisco Transcript, yelled.

"I would answer that question by inviting any of the 'some people' and the men frequenting these places, including you Mr. Jackson, to visit me and I will gladly inform them that most of these girls are underage, brought here by either coercion or against their wills and physically forced into performing illegal acts. They are literally held prisoners and severely punished if they attempt to escape their captors.

"The International Organization for Human Rights estimates there are over twenty million young girls worldwide who are currently forced into this lifestyle and those statistics are confirmed by the FBI and Interpol. So Mr. Jackson, I invite any complaints or suggestions concerning this investigation."

A young woman from a local television channel asked, "Do you believe if the city were to legalize, with strict laws and regulations, prostitution, it would relieve this situation?"

"Well, San Francisco is known for its' diversification and tolerance and I believe your question should be seriously considered. I will encourage the Mayor's office to appoint a committee to consider the pros and cons of just such a proposal," Kane replied.

Before taking the next question, Kane glanced around the room at the crowd of reporters and said, "I believe the more important questions should be, "Where is the outrage? Where are our elected representatives and where is the cry from the so called 'woman's movement' against this? Why has this issue not been addressed by you in the press? I challenge everyone here to do your job. Bring the truth to your readers and listeners. Together we can put an end to the torture and suffering of so many young women and girls."

The questioning and the press conference went on for another half an hour before Kane said, "I'd like to thank the media for your questions and I'm sorry, but I must get back to work."

She walked off the stage and as she entered the adjoining room her assistant handed her a phone and said, "It's Mr. Rusk."

She took the phone and said, "Mr. Rusk, what's up?"

"Well, first of all, let me congratulate your press conference performance and also thank you for your cooperation with the FBI investigation," Rusk commented.

She had long since not questioned how Rusk managed to know everything, but that he had already seen the press conference caused her pause and then she reminded herself, he is a spook.

He continued, "I wanted to inform you that D-day is fast approaching and you can tell Ms. Dinosa she will personally be the person to put the cuffs on the Huang Tong people."

"I appreciate that and I'm sure she'll be tickled to hear it," Kane replied.

—

"Here's to old times and another successful mission," Ian said raising his glass of beer and toasting the other members of his team gathered around a buddy table in Zack's Bar and Grill.

"Well, drink up Nancy, we have a long drive in front of us," Steve said.

Nancy drained her beer, looked sadly at the others and groaned, "Ah, it'll be good to get home, but we're going to miss you guys."

She stood up and hugged in turn, Ian, Grant and Jesse.

"We're going to miss you guys too," Grant said and looking at Ian with a wry grin he added, "But I have a feeling it won't be long before we'll be seeing you again."

After the Cromwell's had departed, Jesse said, "My guess is, our next assignment won't require the abilities of Nancy and Steve."

As if on cue, Ian's phone rang and after a brief conversation he hung up and said, "I guess we're about to find out what that's going to be. We have been summoned to the O'Farrell castle."

—

Mary Dinosa and Joan Richards sat across from one another at a table located on the far side of the bar in the corner inside 'Lefty's Tavern'. They were both nursing a Pilsner Ale.

"Well, I've been informed we'll be busting the big dogs soon. My boss says I'll have the privilege of putting the cuffs on Joey Wang and Billy Choo. Would you like to accompany me?" Dinosa asked.

"I'd love to, but I'd need permission from my boss," Richards replied.

"My boss is very persuasive so I think we can make that happen," Dinosa said with a smirk.

"You know, it's kind of ironic. From since I can remember, I've always wanted to be in law enforcement and I thought the FBI was the golden apple. I've been with the Bureau for five years now and I still feel like the proverbial mushroom. Give me some advice. I know you've earned your stripes, but how did you do it? How did you get in the position to know everything?" Richard said sincerely.

Dinosa snickered and replied, "Its happened mostly by luck, I've bent the rules sometimes, oh hell, I've ignored the rules at times, but if it produces positive results, people will generally overlook how you achieved them. It also helps if you have someone covering your ass, and I've had plenty of those, but if you think I know everything, think again. I've learned sometimes, knowing everything is not such a good idea."

She changed the subject and continued, "I know you interviewed the twins. What did you learn?"

Richards flipped her bangs back, ran her hand through her hair and said, "Ah Geez, what a sad story. They were both at an electronics game arcade with friends not far from their homes in Akron, Ohio. They believe someone slipped something in their cold drinks because the next thing they remember they woke up naked in a flea bag motel in bed with a couple of black guys. This was confirmed by the video recording from the arcade that saw them leave on the arms of the two men. The bad news is, the video quality wasn't good enough to identify their kidnappers. The good news is, we showed them a photo line-up and they each separately identified the two guys."

Richards paused and took a long drink from her beer glass and continued, "For the next two days they were held captive in the motel, sexually molested, fed pills and shot up with heroin. We subsequently learned the motel was across the street from a truck stop just outside Indianapolis, Indiana."

"After several days of captivity, they were put out to turn tricks in the truck stop parking lot. About a week later another man showed up at the motel and for the next year he and sometimes several other pimps traveled with the girls to truck stops along Interstate Eighty until they eventually ended up in your city."

"How prevalent is this problem here in the States?" Dinosa asked.

"You won't believe it, but several studies conducted by reputable organizations, including the FBI, say people enslaved today in the United States outnumber the slave population at the end of the trans-Atlantic slave trade era in the sixteenth and seventeenth centuries. Most of these are women and over fifty percent are minors," Richards sighed.

"What will happen to the Smith cousins?" Dinosa inquired.

"I can't answer that except to say they are in good hands now. Their parents had already reached out to a nonprofit organization called the 'Polaris Project'. One of the services they offer is counseling and comfort to victims like Janis and Sharon. I'm told they have had great success, but the scars of their experiences will be with them a lifetime," Richards responded.

Dinosa found herself making the sign of the cross and whispered, "God willing." She added, "Joan, you will definitely be there when we bust these bastards."

—

"Damn, you dog faces heal almost as fast as us jar heads," Jesse said as he greeted Gary Brown at the entrance to the O'Farrell residence and gave him a hug.

Brown winced and backing away groaned, "Ah, maybe not," and then retorted with a grin, "but we're smart enough to give ourselves enough time to heal."

Grant welcomed him with a handshake and said, "It's good to see you."

"Come on in," Ian said and continued, "The others are downstairs in the planning room."

Ian led them to an elevator located on the far side of the room and they descended to the basement. Exiting the elevator, Brown's eyes widened and he beamed, "Wow, what a set up."

The large room was a gymnasium many college's would be proud to call their own. One end consisted of a regulation half sized basketball court and the other end held a full sized boxing ring in one corner and a large wrestling mat and work out area in the other. A running catwalk circled the room's perimeter.

"Yeah, my father believed in physical fitness for all the family and guests," Ian remarked.

"Well, this will certainly help with my rehab treatment," Brown said.

"I hope four days will be enough time to get you in shape," Ian smirked.

The four men walked across the basketball court and entered an office off of the gymnasium. Tacked to the far wall was a series of four satellite photographs measuring two feet by two feet. Beginning on the left the photographs showed a desert area and each photograph showed the same area and progressively enlarged with a red 'X' in the center. The first map showed Interstate Route 40 where it intersected with Highway 68 from Bullhead City, Nevada at Kingman, Arizona in the top right corner.

The last photograph was an enlarged map of the 'X' marked area and showed what appeared to be a rock and sand quarry. Placing his index finger on the 'X', Ian said, "This is where we'll be in four days."

Directing their attention to a flat screen monitor on another wall, Ian continued, "This is the horizontal view from position 'X', where we believe our targets will be. It is an abandoned rock and sand quarry located in the desert approximately ten miles south of Kingman, Arizona."

"We are now looking almost due north from that position," Ian said and as he zoomed in with a remote control to a sandy knoll dotted with scrub oak trees, he continued, "The top of this rise is about four hundred yards from point 'X' and that's where Jesse and Grant will be in position."

He returned the image to normal size and swung the view to the west and stopped when the azimuth read one hundred eighty-five degrees and showed a small rise in the desolate desert that he zoomed in on.

"This is where Brown and I will be. It's about five hundred yards from the target. Both teams will be armed with the latest version of the MX110 sniper rifle. Brown will spot for me and Grant will do the same for Jesse. Now, let's get down to the particulars," Ian said, passing out manila folders to each man.

Two hours later Ian sighed and said, "We'll have plenty of time to review the plan and your input is welcomed." Glancing at his wrist watch he smiled and said, "It looks like its beer thirty."

The group retired to the deck attached to the rear of the residence that overlooked the large Olympic sized swimming pool. Jesse grabbed four bottles of beer from the refrigerator behind the wet bar and joined his friends around an umbrella table.

After taking a large gulp from his beer, Brown said, "Hmm, you know I've been following the actions of this team for some time and I must say I'm a bit envious and impressed."

"How would you feel about joining us?" Ian asked.

"I'd love to, but let's see what Bernie has to say about that," Brown replied.

—

PART II
'Tham'
Rough Thai translation; Justice

CHAPTER EIGHT

(Three days ago)

"How can we be sure this is not a trap? You steal my money and then you steal my hookers. Tell me why I should trust you now," Joey Wang asked.

He was on the phone with Jamal Franks.

"First of all, I didn't steal your money and one of my hot headed Captains stole your girls in retaliation for the deaths of two of his people in New York he blamed on your people. He has been dealt with. I believe we need a face to face to first discuss our differences before it escalates into a full blown war," Franks replied.

"When my funds are returned, I'll think about it," Wang said.

"Listen, my dear friend, we did not steal your money. The money in our off shore account is also missing and even though the records trace it to one of your accounts, I don't think you were responsible. I believe someone is trying to put a wedge between us and I should have the evidence when we meet next week," Franks explained.

Wang leaned back in his chair and stared at the ceiling in thought.

"Joey, are you still there…?" Franks asked tweaking his neck.

"Yes, I'm just thinking. I know you've heard about the unfortunate deaths of Chon Gai and some of his associates including our Ronald and Roselyn Bingham in Hong Kong. Perhaps someone is positioning themselves to take over our enterprises," Wang said.

"I have heard about Gai and the others, not to mention I've received word that some of my associates in the Middle East and the Ukraine have also been assassinated. I am gathering intelligence and that is why it is imperative we meet," Franks said.

"Okay, but the security protocol will be the same. Neither of us will exit our vehicles until our men have cleared the site and we will meet at the rock and sand quarry," Wang demanded.

"I agree, and I'm also going to have a chopper clear the surrounding area," Franks said.

"Jamal, we have been doing business together for a long time, so don't fuck this up," Wang warned.

"Don't worry about that and I'll see you in a week," Franks replied.

—

(The present)

Dinosa and Richards with their side arms drawn and bullet resistant vests on stood crouched behind a group of a combined FBI and SFPD SWAT team in the driveway leading to the large Victorian style home off Portola Boulevard in the Westwood Highlands District of San Francisco. They watched other members of the SWAT team as they climbed fences and encircled the residence.

Dinosa whispered, "Isn't this a little overkill?"

"Nope, we've got a federal no knock warrant and we're going to teach these fuckers a big lesson," Richards replied.

"I think I'm falling in love with you," Dinosa chuckled.

A smile and a wink from Richards were followed by a loud bang as a manual battering ram knocked in the front door and they began moving forward. Bellows of, "Federal agents, get on the floor and don't move!" could be heard throughout the house.

The two women entered the home and as they moved through it house lights were coming on and several people appearing to be house servants were laying on the floor with an officer standing over them. They followed four officers as they descended the stairs to the basement.

Again they heard a loud voice in front of them yell, "Federal agents, everybody on the ground and don't move!"

The large room was dimly lit and the screams of both men and women could be heard. One of the agents flicked on an overhead light revealing a scene Dinosa had only read about in mid-evil romance novels. The basement was decorated as a prison chamber of the same era. Steel cages lined one wall and two young Asian girls were shackled naked facing the wall with their hands above their heads in a corner. Another blond woman dressed in a crotch less leather one piece swim suit with a leather ski mask dangled from a swing, her legs and arms tied spread eagle. As the other people in the room quieted down and assumed the prone position, a small man dressed only in a matching studded black leather vest and thong and a leather mask covering his face and head, gripping a horse crop approached the first agent and demanded, "What's going on here! I own this home and this is a private party of consenting adults."

"Drop the weapon sir, and get on the ground!" the agent bellowed.

"You have no right..." the little man snarled when the agent grabbed the man's arm holding the whip, kicked him behind his knee and he crumbled to the ground with a scream.

Dinosa looked at Richards and chuckled, "This is the type of fun I'm talk'n about."

She marched over to the little man now lying prone and face down on the floor, reached down and pealed the mask off his face.

"Why Councilman Reid, how strange to see you here, and isn't that your lovely wife the officers are helping untie from that swing?" Dinosa said with surprise sarcasm as the officer pulled the mask off of the struggling woman's head.

The little man covered his face with his hands and Dinosa gave him more than a nudge with her boot to his ribs and ordered, "Arms straight out with your palms down!" and added, "Now be a good little boy, Dickie."

Richards and another female officer were unlatching the two Asian girls from the wall and she noticed red welts covered their backs and buttocks. They covered the girls with blankets before walking them to a mattress and gently sitting them down. The two girls were shivering, their wide eyes dancing around in terror and confusion.

Richards looked at them sadly and said consolingly, "Its' okay girls. Don't be frightened, we're here to help you."

A group of EMTs arrived and began taking the girl's vital signs. They gently laid them on stretchers and carried them upstairs and outside to awaiting ambulances. Dinosa glanced around the room and saw about fifteen people in various stages and manner of dress lying on the floor. It appeared there was an equal mix of sexes but they all had one thing in common. They all looked extremely frightened.

The SWAT team leader approached her and said, "The transport wagons are waiting outside. Should we allow these people a change of clothes before loading them?"

Dinosa set her chin and gritted her teeth, "Nope, too much of a security risk wouldn't you say?"

"Yes Ma'am, I agree," the Officer said with a knowing grin.

She produced her cell phone and dialed the SFPD media relations Officer and said, "Yes, this is D.A. Investigator Mary Dinosa. I want you to alert all of the local media outlets and tell them they'd be wise to get their camera crews to police headquarters ASAP. Tell them we've arrested some high profile citizens including City Councilman Richard Reid."

"A good old perp walk?" an astonished Richards commented.

"I think they've earned it, don't you?" Dinosa replied tilting her head.

"You can't do this," Reid whined, "I'll have your job!"

Dinosa nudged him with her boot in the ribs again and barked, "Shut up, you little mutt."

"Ah shit, I think I'm falling in love with you," Richards giggled.

—

Jesse and Grant approached the bleachers set up in front of an open meadow of tall grass, shrub oak trees and a variety of other small growth bushes and behind a sign that posted, 'USMC Field Camouflage and Detection Course, Camp Pendleton'. A gruff looking lean and mean Marine with Gunnery Sergeant chevrons on his sleeves stood to one side of the bleachers on a platform. Approximately fifty recruits sat in the stands.

"I want all of you to keenly observe the scenery before you. There are six United States Marine expert snipers out there with their rifle trained on you and about to kill you!" he bellowed.

"Now, you have all been issued pen light laser pointers. I want each of you to locate one of the enemy and aim your lasers at him!" he ordered.

Red dots began to appear at various targets throughout the meadow. A dozen or so appeared on what appeared to be a fallen tree trunk about fifty yards out. The sergeant pointed his laser at the target, jiggled his dot up and down and said, "By a show of hands, who picked this target?"

Twelve arms raised. "Congratulations, boots, you just killed an age old, priceless petrified manzanita bush."

Turning back toward the meadow he roared, "Marine snipers, show yourselves!"

One by one the snipers began rising. After five of them, camouflaged with floral decorated body netting, revealed themselves without a single red dot on them, the sergeant yelled, "Corporal Robinson, did you not hear me?"

"Yes, Gunnery Sergeant Kelly, I heard you," a loud voice replied as a mesquite bush not five yards from him and ten yards from the bleachers rose out of the sand to reveal a soldier with his AR16 rifle trained on the recruits.

Grunts of 'ah shit' and 'son of a bitch' from the recruits was interrupted by applause coming from Jesse and Grant who were now standing next to the bleachers.

Kelly glanced over at the two and roared, "What miscreant mother fuckers are interrupting my class?"

"Whoa Gunny, we're just showing our appreciation," Grant chuckled.

Kelly squinted his eyes, tilted his head and with a wide grin said, "We'll if it ain't fuck'n Amos and Andy," and turning back toward the recruits he bellowed, "Okay, boots, take five and smoke 'em if you got 'em."

He joined the two and after sharing a hug he asked, "What the hell brings you two old ground pounders here?"

"Well, as the best sniper and camouflage man this Corp has ever seen," Jesse began, "We were hoping you could give us a little advice."

"I heard you two had quit the Corp and the scuttlebutt has it your some kind of mercenaries now," Kelly said.

"Well, we did resign from the Corp, but we have assimilated nicely into civilian life and the scuttlebutt is just bull shit," Jesse replied.

"Right, and that's why two nice assimilated civilians are here seeking my advice," Kelly drawled with sarcasm.

"As I recall, I carried your skinny ass through the jungles of Somalia one day," Grant reminded him.

"Yeah, it wouldn't hurt to share a pitcher of beer and swap some old war stories. Why don't we hook-up at the NCO Club, let's say about 1700 hours," Kelly said.

Walking back toward their car Jesse commented, "Jesus Christ, are we just getting old or did those recruits look like they were just cut loose from their momma's apron strings."

"Both," Grant chuckled.

—

Dinosa and Richards were traveling south on the Bay Shore Freeway in Dinosa's fifteen year old Subaru Outback. The seats were well worn and the plastic dash cover was beginning to crack. The back seat was littered with candy wrappers, empty soda cans and water bottles and Richards wondered God only knows what else.

"Jesus Mary, I know you're just a lowly public servant, but doesn't the city pay you enough to buy a new car like every decade or so?" Richards complained.

"I'm sentimentally attached to old 'Helga'. I've had her since the academy and I've become attached," Dinosa commented.

'Helga, you named your car?" Richards said with amazement.

"Yeah, I named her after my high school student advisor. We called her 'Helga the Witch'. You should see my other car. It's a 1964 Volkswagen bus painted psychedelically," Dinosa snickered.

"That's rich," Richards said rolling her eyes.

"Okay, tell me more about this Saint Leo's Sanctuary House you're taking me to," Dinosa said turning serious.

"It's a home for wayward young women and girls in San Jose who either have no other place to go or are waiting to be reunited with their families. It's sponsored by the Catholic Church and run by the Sisters of Notre Dame.

"I thought you'd be interested in meeting the young Latino girls who were brought here from south of the border and forced into a life of prostitution on the streets and in sleazy motels," Richards replied.

"Sounds like a cheery little outing," Dinosa whined.

"Mary, these girls are like the ones you've been rescuing from the filthy sex traders in your city and like the ones that washed up on your beaches. They're like the Smith cousins who are among the hundreds of girls who are kidnapped or lured off of our own streets every year. Actually Mary, I wanted you to see what keeps me going," Richards sighed.

They drove on in silence until Richards said, "You want to take this exit."

She directed Dinosa through the downtown San Jose area and into a commercial warehouse development. At one intersection a group of scantily clad females, ranging in various ages and colors, stood on one corner and several of them bent down in sexy poses to peer into Dinosa's window as the two women drove by.

Several turns later they entered a residential neighborhood and Richard directed Dinosa to pull into a parking lot across the street from two three story buildings separated by an entrance with the simple sign above the double doors saying 'Saint Leo's'.

Upon entering the building they were met by a rosy cheeked, gregarious middle aged woman dressed in Nun's habit.

"Oh Joan, it's so good to see you again. I saw you walking across the street from my office window and wanted to personally greet you," she said while hugging Richards.

"It's good to see you too," Richards reciprocated and turning toward Dinosa added, "I'd like you to meet a friend and colleague of mine. Mary Dinosa, meet Sister Madelyn. She's the HNIC, or should I say she's the head Nun in charge here."

"It's nice to meet you," the Sister said shaking Dinosa's hand.

"Likewise," Dinosa replied.

Turning back toward Richards, the Sister said, "Since your call, I've asked several of the girls if they'd be willing to talk to you and they've agreed. They're waiting now in the court yard."

The three walked across the foyer and through another set of double doors into an open atrium and a garden of blooming roses, chrysanthemums, tulips and green shrubbery. A path led to a patio and table where three young Latino women were seated. As they approached, the three girls all stood up.

Mary thought sadly, my God these girls are beautiful and should be preparing themselves for their high school proms, but she superficially smiled and beamed when they were introduced.

"Mary and Joan, I'd like you to meet three of our residents. This is Anna Sanchez and these are sisters Maria and Gabriella Lopez. Please, help yourselves to the iced tea and I'll leave you alone to chat," Sister Madelyn said after filling two glasses with iced tea before leaving.

Richards began, "I'm so grateful you have been brave enough to talk to us and realize how important it is for us to understand how it was you found yourselves here so together we can prevent this from happening to other young girls."

Anna Sanchez bowed her head and then lifting it and looking at the sisters, she said, "It will be difficult, but since I've been the longest one here, I will start," she said speaking slowly with a heavy Spanish accent, but concise and understandable.

She related that she had migrated from Guatemala about four years ago. She came with an older brother and human smugglers called 'coyotes', for a price of five hundred American dollars, led them across the border into Mexico. Their plan was to get to the United States and meet up with a cousin in Nogales, Arizona, and work on a ranch where their cousin was employed.

They were transported to Juarez, Mexico, and handed off to another man who separated her from her brother. She was told she would have to work selling her body on the streets of Juarez to earn her passage to America or she would be tortured and killed. That is when they started giving her daily injections of heroin. She was thirteen years old. She believes about six months later she was herded with about eight other young girls through a tunnel and when they emerged in a bedroom closet, they were told they were in the United States.

They spent that night in the house she had emerged in and the very next day they were transported in a semi-truck to Phoenix, Arizona, where she spent the next year or so as a prostitute working truck stops and sleazy motels in the area. From there she was taken to San Jose to work the streets.

One night she was picked up by a couple and thought they wanted three-way sex. Instead, they brought and dropped her off at Saint Leo's. Sister Madelyn and other Nuns took her in and explained that she didn't have to live that way anymore. They were her saviors. She had been there a little over one year.

Dinosa asked, "So what will happen to you now?"

"The Sisters have taught me English and I attend job training classes to become an office receptionist. Sister Madelyn is working on getting me a green card and I've already been offered a job. Eventually, I'd like to become a U.S. citizen and become a translator, but as the Sisters tell me, one step at a time."

Maria and Gabriella had similar stories. When asked if they remembered anything about their captors the only thing they agreed on was they referred to themselves as 'La Guardia'. The meeting lasted another hour as the three girls related personal horror stories and how Saint Leo's had been their savior.

As they pulled out of the parking lot, Dinosa turned toward Richards and asked curiously, "You were a resident there once, weren't you?"

"Yes, and someday I'll tell you about it."

CHAPTER NINE

"Hah, I can't believe it. This is actually an email from Franks to Wang setting up the protocol and agenda for their upcoming meeting? Franks really is a politician, isn't he?" Ian said incredulously.

He slid the paper across the patio table to Gary Brown. They were on the pool side deck behind the O'Farrell Estate with his father and Solomon Goldsmith. As Brown perused the email, Goldsmith said, "Yep, Grub intercepted it. I, for one, never ask how he does it."

The email subject was 'Proposed Meeting Protocol and Agenda' and read;

Dear Mr. Wang,

Here is what I propose for our upcoming meeting protocol:

The advance teams for both sides should consist of ten, but no more than twelve members. I suggest they arrive at the meeting site at 8:30 a.m. Your team should clear the south side perimeter and set up security and my team will do the same for the north side.

Interested parties should arrive at 8:45 a.m. and set up tables and chairs at the meeting site. I'll have representatives there from Chicago, Kansas City, Cleveland, Minneapolis, Houston, Dallas, New Orleans, Miami and New York City.

You and your staff and mine should arrive at the scheduled 9:00 a.m. meeting time and start the proceedings.

At the conclusion of the meeting I suggest we depart in the reverse order we arrived.

Here is what I propose for the meeting agenda:

1. We begin the meeting by introducing our associates.

2. *Come to agreement that recent hostile actions against both of our organizations were not perpetrated by either of us and discuss who we believe may be conspiring against us. Also patch up any differences we may have which I personally don't believe is good for either party.*
3. *A discussion concerning the recent events of the federal actions on both of our enterprises and make suggestions and plans of action to prevent future intrusions.*
4. *A discussion on our personal exposure to ensure that we are not individually liable for any future criminal prosecution.*
5. *A discussion about the recent attacks on our suppliers overseas and who may be responsible and a plan to ensure that our temporary interruption of product movement, both here and overseas, can be restored.*
6. *An open general discussion on ways we can improve the services we provide to increase our profits.*
7. *Conclude the meeting with handshakes and a commitment to proceed in a manner that will be beneficial to both parties.*

If you have any suggestions to add to this, please let me know and also know that I'm willing to proceed in the spirit of cooperation.

Yours Truly,

Jamal Franks

"Holy shit, if this wasn't so serious it'd be comical. The modern gangster communication, this should be put to rap music and played at the next hip hop concert for Christ's sake," Brown said shaking his head in disgust.

"Well, this should certainly make it easier for you boys to disrupt their little powwow," Sean O'Farrell remarked.

After taking a gulp from his glass of iced tea, Ian looked at his father and said, "Pop, it's never easy."

—

"That may have been the best baked salmon I've ever had and those crab Rangoon appetizers we're the best. I am stuffed," Brown, having been introduced by Ian O'Farrell as Bill Gray, said backing away from the table, wiping his mouth with his napkin and then sipping from his glass of wine.

"That was a delicious meal, thanks guys," Joan Richards commented.

The two had joined Ian and Mary at the Neptune's Waterfront Grill and Bar on Pier Thirty-nine on the San Francisco Bay for a delightful fish food meal and companionship.

Dinosa stifled a belch and mumbled, "Oh excuse me," and then added quickly, "Your welcome, this is one of our favorite restaurants."

"Well ladies, why don't you tell us about your day," Ian said.

"Eh, it was pretty routine," Dinosa replied flippantly and then continued in the same manner, "We did bust one of our City's finest politicians."

"Go on…" Brown said leaning forward.

"Oh Mary, you're so modest. One of the top priorities in our investigation is to uncover private citizens who participate in either purchasing or renting these poor girls for their personal sexual gratification and we will prosecute them. You'd be surprised at the number of seemingly normal people who exploit these girls. It's become more and more popular for the so called up scale swinger's set to indulge in this behavior. It's pathetic, and we're frustrated that our bosses won't let us take down the king pins, yet," Richards contributed.

"So Bill, I'm curious as to how you and my dear fiancé met?" Dinosa asked.

Brown glanced at Ian and said, "We first met during the war some years ago and have occasionally kept in touch. I was here on assignment to write a revue of your great city for a travel magazine and decided to look up my old buddy."

Ian waved at the waiter, nodded at him to bring the tab and changing the subject said, "I don't think you'll have to wait much longer to take down the king pins."

Richards glanced curiously at Dinosa and then at Ian and then started to ask, "How would you…"

"Joan, I've learned not to question Ian about what he knows because usually I don't want to know the answer," Dinosa said and then looked at Ian menacingly.

This time Brown interrupted and asked, "Which hotel are you staying at, Joan? I'd love to share a cab with you and maybe we could have an after dinner drink and I'll explain it to you."

Richards raised her eye brows and looking at Brown said, "I'd love an after dinner drink and an explanation."

After Ian paid the bill the foursome left the restaurant and walked down the pier toward the Embarcadero Center. Dinosa accompanied their two companions to a cab and said good night as Ian handed his stub to a parking valet.

When the car arrived they got in and as Ian pulled onto the Embarcadero Boulevard, Dinosa turned toward him and scowled, "What the hell was that all about?"

"What was what all about?" Ian asked innocently.

"You know damned well what that was all about," Dinosa growled and then muttered, "Oh shit, I'm starting to sound like my mother."

"If you're referring to my comment that you won't have to wait much longer, I thought she earned the right to know," Ian replied calmly.

"And what about me, when were you going to tell me?" Dinosa fumed.

"Listen Mary, both Gary and I thought you both deserved to have your minds put at ease. The little I now about Joan Richards isn't much, but I have heard she's put her heart and soul into this and, by the way, you and I haven't had a lot of face to face time lately."

"Gary? I thought his name was Bill?" Dinosa asked offensively.

"Okay, William Gray is not his real name," Ian admitted, "but everything else he said was true, except why he's in San Francisco." Ian winced at this final revelation.

"I know, it's one of those things I don't need or want to know," Dinosa whined.

—

Ian walked out of the registration office at the Fort Beale RV Park located just off Interstate 40 in Kingman, Arizona, and climbed into the idling thirty foot RV parked out front.

"We're in the last spot on the right," he told Brown who was behind the wheel.

They were followed down the lane by an F150 jet black Ford pickup towing a flatbed trailer with two dune buggies latched to its' bed. Grant was driving and Jesse sat in the passenger seat. They pulled up next to the RV at their designated hook-up spot and exited the vehicle.

Grant reacted to the intense heat after leaving the air conditioned confines of the truck's cab and mumbled, "Jesus Christ it's hot."

As they walked toward the side door of the RV, an older couple sitting at a picnic table under the roll out awning of their travel trailer waived at them and the white haired man dressed in striped bermuda shorts with black loafers and knee high black socks hollered from the adjacent space, "Welcome neighbors!"

They returned the wave and met Ian at the door as he was leaving the RV and Grant said, "Where you going man, it's hotter than hell out here?"

"Well, if you two geniuses want to stay cool, someone has to hook-up this rig to electricity," Ian replied sarcastically.

"Oh yeah, you need any help?" Grant asked.

"Naw."

"Good," Grant replied with relief as he followed Jesse inside.

A few minutes later Ian appeared at the door and seeing his three friends sitting around the small dining table all drinking a cold soda, said, "Don't get too comfortable guys. We need to get out to the site and make a run through."

They piled into the pick-up truck and traveled southwest out of Kingman on Interstate Route 40. About five miles later they turned off of the Interstate and continued in the same direction on State Route 10 until they came to a dusty dirt road and made a right turn.

Several miles later they came to a dry rocky creek bed that wound north and disappeared behind a desert knoll. "This must be the spot where we hide the truck and trailer. Pull up this creek bottom and around that rise," Ian told Grant.

They drove up the gulley far enough to satisfy themselves they were out of view from the road, stopped and exited the vehicle. While Grant and Jesse off loaded the dune buggies, Ian and Brown were unfolding a large camouflaged tarp they had retrieved from a truck bed utility box. Soon Grant and Jesse joined them and they spread the tarp over the truck and trailer.

Inspecting their work, Jesse remarked, "It looks good to me."

"Okay," Ian started, consulting a satellite map, "the quarry is located about eight miles up the road and tomorrow you guys will peel off here and continue northwest to this point north of the target area. We'll be taking this route," he continued pointing out a location, "and take up position at this spot south of the target. Today we're going to make a dress rehearsal and then meet at the target area. Let's plug in our ear wigs for a communication check."

After the check was completed, Ian said, "Grab and check your gear and let's roll."

They returned to the utility box at the back of the truck and each man grabbed a back pack and put them on. Ian and Jesse retrieved M40A sniper rifles. Each weapon was equipped with a muzzle break and sound suppressor and a detachable scope with range finder. Grant and Brown grabbed AR16 fully automatic rifles.

Jesse and Grant jumped into one of the buggies and sped off up the dry creek bed. They followed the winding gulley until they stopped below a rise on their left. "This must be the spot," Jesse said.

They retrieved their weapons from scabbards in the back of the buggy, covered it with a camouflaged tarp and ascended the sandy rise. When they reached the top, Grant was perspiring profusely and gasped, "Damn, it's hot."

Below them they could see the road ended at a large flat area butted up against the excavated side of a mesa that led to the Sierra Mountains on the distant western horizon.

"I see you're in position," cackled in their ear pieces.

They both looked across the flat area and could see Brown and Ian waving their arms atop another rise some one thousand yards from their position. "Yeah, we see you," Grant said.

"Okay, dress up and take your positions. I'm going to circle around and get to the top of the mesa for a look see," Ian announced.

"Ah piss, it's hot enough without getting into that bogeyman suit," Grant complained.

"I heard that," Ian chuckled and added, "You're getting too fat and lazy. Quit whining like a little girl."

Jesse was taking off his back pack and doubled over giggling. He gathered his wits and pulled a netting robe from his pack. Flaring it out, he laid it on the ground, stepped back and said, "Old Gunny Kelly sure knows his shit."

It was hard to distinguish where the robe ended and the ground started. He slipped the garb on and adjusted it until he was comfortable and laid down facing the quarry. He used his back pack as a gun rest and after slipping a camouflaged cover over the barrel of his M40A rifle barrel, he took aim at his pretend target.

"How do I look?" Grant asked.

Jesse glanced back at him and chuckled, "Like a giant camel turd."

"Fuck you," Grant mumbled as he lay down next to his friend and then grumbled, "Hey Ian, where the hell are you? I'm boiling down here."

"I'm almost there. Let me know when you're medium rare. That's how I like my black meat," Ian replied with a snicker.

"Fuck you too," Grant retorted good naturedly.

Ian had dropped off Brown at their designated spot and then drove the buggy back and around the mesa and was approaching the eastern end. He parked the buggy and walked to the cliff edge of the mesa and looked down through a pair of binoculars. He first looked to where Grant and Jesse should be and seeing nothing out of the ordinary he shifted his view to where Brown should be.

"Okay snipers, pick a target and on the count of three, fire one shot," Ian said and paused for a moment before saying, "Three, two, one."

He could not distinguish between the two almost inaudible pops. He saw two puffs of dust rise from the desert floor.

"Perfect," he said.

When they returned to the RV park, the four men grabbed their shaving kits and a towel and headed toward the common men's shower and restroom located in the center of the park. The sun was just setting on the horizon and the day had cooled somewhat when they shower room activities and departed the building.

As they passed the trailer parked adjacent to theirs, the older man was busy in front of the barbeque pit cooking hamburger patties and said, "Hey, why don't you boys join the wife and me for a burger? They say I make the meanest greasy cheeseburger in Arizona."

They all looked at one another and Grant beamed, "Sounds great and thanks. Can you give us a minute?"

"Not a problem," the white haired man replied.

When they joined their dinner hosts, the woman was setting down a bowl of potato salad on the picnic table and looked up smiling.

Flipping a burger, the old man said, "Meet my wife Martha. My name is Will, it's nice to meet you gentlemen."

Grant was carrying a cooler and asked, "Ma'am, where would you like me to put this?"

"Oh, just anywhere," Martha replied.

After introductions were made, Jesse opened the cooler and asked, "Anybody care for a cold beer?"

"Oh, no thank you. I prefer my wine," Martha said, reaching down and picking up a half filled drinking glass. All of the men accepted his offer.

"You boys look pretty clean cut. If I had to guess, I'd say you're all military," Will commented.

"Ex-military," Ian said, "Gary was a dog face and Grant and Jesse were jar heads. I was a swabbie."

"Well, thank you all for your service," Will said, raising his bottle of beer in a toast.

"How about you?" Brown asked.

"I was in the Army and, in fact, I met my beautiful wife when she patched me up after I was wounded in Viet Nam. She was a nurse in the Woman's Army Corp," Will replied.

Jesse raised his bottle and said, "Well sir, thank you two for your service."

Will turned away and cleared his voice. A moment later he turned around and with red eyes said, "I'm sorry, but you're the first man that has ever thanked me for my service. When we came home we were spit on and called baby killers. Hell, I enlisted in the Army to serve and protect my country just like my father and his father did. I sure as hell didn't think I'd come home and be treated like a second class citizen and some sort of a traitor and I should apologize. Kinda puts a sour taste in your mouth, you know."

"Sir, the nation owes you and your fellow soldiers an apology," Grant said solemnly.

Will laid a platter of burgers patties covered with melted cheese and mushrooms down on the table and jubilated, "Dig in boys!"

The rest of the evening was filled with drinking beer, jokes and laughter as the group swapped old war stories and reminisced about their time in the service.

As the group was breaking up, Grant bellowed, "Martha that was the best potato salad I ever had, and Will, whoever said you make the meanest cheeseburger in Arizona was right on. Thank you very much."

Martha pulled Ian aside and whispered, "I'd like to thank you and your friends. Tonight was the first time I ever heard Willie talk about the war."

"No ma'am, we owe you the thanks. It was our privilege."

—

Jamal Franks sat across from his old friend from the hood and chief body guard, Mohammed Aljabar. They were traveling south on State Route 10, in the back of a cream colored Cadillac limousine that was following two black SUVs. He picked up his cell phone and dialed Joey Wang's number and put his phone on speaker mode.

"Hello my friend, it's Jamal. I assume you are on time."

Wang replied, "Yes, we are approaching the quarry road."

"I suggest we both stop and wait here and allow our teams to continue to the meeting place and clear the area. My helicopter is overhead as we speak to ensure we have a private meeting," Franks said.

"I must warn you, half of my team is already there. Since you were the one who set up this meeting, I thought it would only be wise for my people to prescreen the area. It's purely precautionary and I hope you understand," Wang said.

A concerned look crossed Franks' face and he looked at Aljabar who merely shrugged and muttered, "Eh."

"Of course I understand your concern," Franks replied and added, "but if anything should go south at this meeting, I guarantee your ashes in an urn will be leading the Chinese New Year's parade."

"Understood," Wang retorted with a snort as he hung up and watched Franks' limousine pull up and park on the road's shoulder across from the SUV he sat in.

As the limousine pulled up and parked on the shoulder, the two SUVs it was following continued after making a left turn and sped down the quarry road.

Franks' phone rang and he picked up.

"Mr. Franks, this is Charles in the helicopter. I see six men who look Asian. They're standing beside a black SUV about twenty yards north of a table and chairs in the middle of the flat area."

"That's okay, how about the surrounding area?" Franks replied.

"The perimeter is clear for about a five mile radius," Charles reported.

"Fine, you can return to your heliport now."

The two sniper teams were in position on the rises to the north and south of the meeting place. They lay prone and concealed beneath their camouflaged nets and had been in place since just after sunrise. In the previous hour, they watched as a black SUV pulled into the flat area below their position and six Asian men exited the vehicle and busied themselves with setting up a folding table and chairs. They were now standing around smoking cigarettes and chatting amongst themselves. The helicopter, that had been circling the area, made one more pass and then swooped away to the east.

A few minutes passed and three more SUVs pulled into the area and one parked behind the SUV to the north and the other two to the south. The occupants of the newly arrived vehicles exited and the two sides of twelve men lined up facing each other about fifty feet apart.

"Looks like high noon at the OK corral," Jesse quipped into his lapel microphone.

"Well boys, you're about to witness two groups of gangbangers blow each other away," Ian commented.

"It just doesn't get any better than this. Who brought the popcorn?" Grant commented.

"You got your target sighted?" Ian asked.

"Roger," Jesse replied.

"On the count of three, two, one…" Two pops rang out and a gangbanger from each side went down.

Immediately, men from each side produced their weapons and started firing at each other. Some had small fully automatic pistol grip rifles and others had semi-automatic hand guns. The canyon filled with the sounds of weapons erupting and the screams of men getting hit and dying. Within a minute, most of the men lay dead or writhing in agony on the ground. One man from each side could be seen running in opposite directions. Two more pops rang out and the two men fell face first in in a cloud of dust.

Parked on the side of Route ten, Wang's SUV lurched forward, peeled out and sped away heading south.

"You mother fucker? Let's get out of here!" Franks yelled at his driver.

CHAPTER TEN

"Hey George, its Bernie, I wanted to congratulate you and your team on another successful mission. I just witnessed live on a satellite feed, what I'm going to call the 'Gangbanger Mojave Massacre'," Bernard Rusk spoke into his phone from the Situation Room at CIA headquarters in Langley, Virginia.

"Thank you Bernard and I'll be sure to share that with the others," George Armstrong said, giving the thumbs up sign to Sean O'Farrell and Solomon Goldsmith who were gathered with him in the den of his Los Gatos home.

"Can you put me on speaker? I'd like to bring you guys up to speed on the investigation," Rusk said.

Armstrong complied and laid his phone on the table.

"Go ahead," he prompted.

"Well gentlemen, the Justice Department has arrested, at last count, two hundred and eighty-six people across the nation and more Grand Jury indictments are still coming down in virtually every precinct in the country. These guys are rolling over on one another like a long, long line of dominos. Our partners is Canada have reported similar successes.

"The DOJ has assembled a team comprised of over one hundred of our most veteran lawyers and best young legal minds in the country to prosecute these bastards. The headlines in every newspaper and virtually every network and cable news channels are leading with this story," Rusk said gleefully.

"Happy to do our part," Goldsmith responded.

"Oh don't be so modest Sol. We never could have done it without you and your team," Rusk replied and then his mood turned serious when he continued, "We still have a traffic problem coming from south of the border. We need to nip that in the bud while we've got the buyers up here on the run and before another distribution network can be set up. We're going to need your team for that."

"We're standing by," O'Farrell said.

"Oh, by the way, a little fairy told me some hacker transferred about two billion dollars from a couple of off shore bank accounts to an account we can't trace. I guess it's the old 'finder's keepers, loser's weepers' scenario. I'm sure the finders will put it to good use. At least to better use than our Treasury Department would," Rusk snickered.

"What's going to happen to the girls? Will they be deported?" Goldsmith asked.

"Absolutely not," Rusk said and continued, "With all the publicity and public outcry this story has generated, the Administration doesn't have the stomach to send these girls back. They'll be taken to local hospitals for a medical evaluation and treatment and after their release they'll be transported to a facility in New Mexico that was originally constructed for the anticipated influx of World War II foreign refugees from the Pacific and East Asia. After counseling and treatment they'll be placed in appropriate foster homes or group homes and hopefully be assimilated into society. Those who sincerely wish to return to their homelands will be given free passage."

"So when will we be heading south?" O'Farrell asked.

"Soon, Sean, very soon," Rusk answered.

That morning's headline atop page one in the Phoenix Daily Sun read;

TWENTY-FOUR BODIES FOUND FIFTEEN MILES SOUTHWEST OF KINGMAN AS A RESULT OF APPARENT GANG SHOOTOUT

The ensuing story started;

Responding to calls of shots fired, County Sheriff's Deputies discovered twenty-four bullet riddled deceased bodies at an abandoned sand and gravel quarry approximately ten miles west of Route Ten and south of Kingman early yesterday afternoon.

Motive for the murders were unknown but a Sheriff's Department Spokesman said, "Twelve of the victims appeared to be young Asian Americans and the same amount appeared to be African Americans. We can only speculate at this time that some sort of a gang related dispute erupted between these two groups. We are conducting an ongoing investigation."

Identification of the victims has not been released and authorities have said the FBI has been called in to assist with the investigation...

Two armored trucks marked SFPD SWAT pulled up outside the 'Chinese Dragon' restaurant on Grant Street in Chinatown and the eight man teams filed out of the back of each vehicle. Police cruisers blocked traffic at opposing intersections and cleared access for waiting EMS vans. Uniformed police officers were busy clearing the sidewalks of civilian foot traffic. Several SWAT members moved down the alley separating the restaurant from the adjacent building and covered the rear. The rest of the team grouped at a door next to the restaurant's entrance with Dinosa, Jones and Garner behind them.

Dinosa nodded her head and an officer holding a battering ram slammed it into the door flinging it open. From across the street another officer fired a flash bang grenade through a second story window of the building. The SWAT officers entered single file through the door that led to a flight of stairs.

The lead SWAT member hollered, "San Francisco Police, we have a warrant. Everybody get face down on the floor with your arms out, palms up!"

He continued to repeat the order as the team filed up the stairs, Dinosa close behind. The landing at the top opened into a large conference style room with a table in the center surrounded by chairs, some of which were overturned. Dinosa, Jones and Gardner waited on landing as the team entered the room. Residual smoke and the smell of gun powder from the flash grenades lingered in the air.

"What the hell do you want?" an overweight Asian man lying on the floor groaned.

"Shut up!" the team leader yelled and added, "Clear!"

Dinosa entered the room and identifying Joey Wang she walked over to him and spat out, "Stand up you pig and turn around with your hands up!"

Wang complied and Dinosa patted him down. When she got to his crotch she cupped her hand and squeezed hard. He winced and doubled over and she apologized, saying, "Oops, thought that might be a weapon but it felt like a pecker, only smaller."

She reached down and grabbed one of his hands that was now protecting his manhood and jerked it up and behind him. Slapping a cuff on his wrist and tightening it, she said, "Joey Wang, you are under arrest. You have the right to remain silent and I'll give you the rest of it downtown."

She shoved him toward Jones and Gardner and said, "He's all yours."

Looking around the room at the half a dozen other men sprawled out on the floor she spotted a stunned looking Billy Choo. She walked over to him and noticed his eyes were dull and he was gaping and moving his jaw as if to clear his ears. She kicked his buttocks to gain his attention and when he looked up at her with glazed eyes, she chuckled, "You must have been close to the big boom and flash."

He responded with, "Huh?"

"Never mind," she snickered and turning toward the SWAT leader she said, "Cuff them all and, Pete, thanks to you and your men for an excellent job."

"Our pleasure, Ma'am," Pete said, tipping a finger to his helmet.

Outside, Dinosa approached Jones and Gardner just after they placed Wang in the back seat of a patrol car and smiled at them, "Drinks at Lefty's on me tonight."

"Where the hell is Richards? I thought she wanted to be part of this," Gardner asked.

Dinosa grinned and said, "She was summoned to go to Detroit last night. She took a red eye. I'm guessing she's slapping the cuffs on Jamal Franks right about now."

—

PART III
Gracias, Mucho Gracias

English Translation; 'Thank you, thank you very much.'

CHAPTER ELEVEN

The last moving van pulled away from the circular driveway and disappeared behind the first bend in the private lane that led up the hill from Mary's and Ian's new beach front home.

"Oh God, if I ever suggest or even hint that we should move again, please just fucking shoot me," Dinosa groaned as she plopped down on the still covered sedan that faced the bay window in their new living room overlooking the Pacific Ocean.

The room was still cluttered with unopened crates and boxes. Ian pulled an old lava lamp from a box and sitting down next to her and placing it on the table in front of them, ignoring her previous statement, he beamed, "Wow, this beauty survived another move."

Dinosa wrinkled her nose and pleaded, "Oh Ian, please don't say you want to display that ugly thing in our home."

"But Mary, this has so much sentimental attachment. This was given to me by my mother when I was just a little boy as a night light. She told me it would keep the monsters away," he countered sarcastically.

"Well, it can keep the monsters away in your work shop then. It's my job to keep the monsters away in our bedroom," she said, batting her eyes.

Ian draped his arm around her and pulled her closer and looking out the window, cooed, "Looks like a picture postcard, doesn't it?"

The sun sat like a gymnast's balance ball on the flat Pacific Ocean horizon, casting her orange glow across her domain of the purple sea. They sat together in silence, soaking in and enjoying the marvelous view. After the sun disappeared below the horizon and the skies darkened, Ian rose and turned on an overhead light and said, "I'm going to prepare us a hot bubble bath. You just relax and I'll call you when it's ready."

Mary laid her head back and closed her eyes and drifted off into a warm never-never land somewhere between sleep and total serenity. She lost the concept of time when her blissful state was interrupted.

"Mary, come on its ready!"

Her eyes opened abruptly and she started to panic before reality sat in. She inhaled deeply and sighed before rising and making her way to the hallway where she looked down and was surprised to see a path of red rose petals. She followed them snickering to herself down the hall and into the master bedroom where they ended at the other side of the room at the closed bathroom door. She stripped her clothes off and laid them on the bed and then with anticipation, opened the bathroom door. It was dimly lit with at least a dozen candles surrounding the jumbo sized tub. A smiling Ian sat in the tub with the bubbles covering him from his chest down and he was holding two filled champagne glasses.

She stepped into the tub and sat down between his legs with her back toward him, accepted a glass of champagne and giggled, "Oh Ian, you're such a romantic. What are you going to do when we're old and feeble?"

"Well, I suppose the rose petals will be dried up and faded by then, but I'll build bathroom parking stalls for our walkers and have one of those walk in tubs installed," he said and then, just before dunking her head beneath the bubbles, added, "And the champagne will be prune juice."

Later that night, after a long love making session, they lay in their bed and Dinosa said, "I don't know and don't necessarily want to know what you guys did on your last mission, but I want you to know how much I appreciate it and love you for it."

"The feelings are mutual. I hear you guys did a pretty good job too," Ian replied.

"Well, I know the job isn't done," and she added as an afterthought, "Perhaps it'll never be completely done, but I know there's still the traffic problem from south of the border and knowing you and your group, you have something planned. I want to be included."

"Aha, here it comes. I should have known there was hook," Ian said slapping his head.

"I'm serious. I have an emotional and physical investment in this cause. I'm one of the people who have to deal with these young innocent girls and I've earned the right to see this through," she protested.

Ian sighed and said, "We have a planning meeting tomorrow and I'll see if there's a part for you."

"I have confidence you will," Dinosa smirked.

CHAPTER TWELVE

Arturo Vasquez sat in a patio lounge chair on his large veranda that overlooked the beaches and the Gulf of Mexico waters to the east and his Olympic sized swimming pool to the south. He was a large man with a thick mop of black hair slicked back and a reddish brown, pock scarred face. He was watching his eighteen year old son, Arturo Junior, as the boy and some of his friends surfed the small waves that were breaking on the white sands below.

'Hacienda de la Vasquez' was located at the end of a short driveway off of Bulivar Portaturio on a point about five mile north of the city Heroica Vera Cruz near the southern Mexican border with Guatemala. The sprawling and isolated two story white stucco structure with red adobe tiled roof sat on three acres surrounded by an eight foot brick wall.

Vasquez sat across the table from his wife of almost thirty years, Anna. He was sipping on a Corona beer while she sipped on a glass of iced tea.

"It's good to see the children grow up," Arturo commented in Spanish with a sigh.

"Yes and Junior will be attending the university this year. It's happened so fast. Soon we will be grandparents," Anna replied in their native language.

"Excuse me Senor and Senora Vasquez, but Victor Benitez and another man are at the front door and wish to visit with you Senor Vasquez," a short, middle aged and slightly overweight brown skinned woman dressed in a white cotton dress and standing at the veranda's entrance said contritely.

"That's okay Maria. Please show them up," he answered and gave his wife a knowing nod and she followed Maria back into the house.

A few minutes later he stood up as Victor Benitez and his friend, whom Vasquez recognized as Jorge Batista the head of the El Diablo Cartel, stepped out onto the veranda followed by a very large man dressed in a white cotton suit with a bulge showing on his waist line beneath his jacket. He was Vasquez's personal body guard.

Benitez, Vasquez's right hand man, was a handsome man in his early thirties, of average height, but obviously in good shape. He was dressed in an expensive business suit with a tieless and top unbuttoned white shirt. Batista was similarly dressed but seemed to carry a permanent snarly look below his beady eyes and large nose.

The year before, Vasquez had sent Benitez north to settle the squabbling gang wars that ensued after the assassination of the El Diablo drug cartel leader. Benitez had done his job well and after settling the wars, set up Batista to run the cartel. Vasquez had spent too much time, energy and expense setting up his vast enterprises to allow some punk gang bangers to interfere with it.

His legitimate business was as CEO and President of 'Vasquez Enterprisio', a manufacturer of automobile parts that he exported mainly to American car companies and auto parts suppliers. The bulk of his income came from the illegal sales and distribution of drugs, arms and sex slave trafficking.

He also served on El Presidente's Council for Mexican Economic Growth and held a diplomatic Visa to over thirty countries including the United States. He traveled in a private Lear jet, owned a ninety foot yacht, a chalet in the Swiss Alps and a villa on the French Riviera along with a home in Miami and a penthouse apartment in New York City. He preferred the safe confines of 'Hacienda de la Vasquez' in his mother country and now rarely ventured abroad.

After hugging and welcoming his two visitors he asked, "So Victor, how was your trip north and what can you report?"

"It is not good news, Senor Vasquez," Benitez began, "The recent activities of the gringo federales have resulted in the shutdown of virtually all of our distribution network in their country along with most of our pipelines for transporting the girls across the border.

"The Americano authorities on our payroll have become very nervous and reluctant to cooperate. I'm afraid if we don't reestablish our connections, our profits will take a severe beating."

Vasquez motioned to the large man standing by the veranda's entrance to approach and the man extracted a one page folded piece of paper from his inside breast pocket and handed it to him. Vasquez unfolded it and slid it across the table to Benitez and said, "Read this."

Benitez read to himself;

Dear Senor Vasquez,

For reasons that will become clear I cannot identify myself at this time. Suffice it to say, I'm in the business of sponsoring financially rewarding enterprises much like yourself. I presume 'La Guardia' is having difficulty distributing one of your products in my country and I happen to be in a position to allay that problem.

It will only require that you deliver your product in your country near a pre-designated location in proximity of our mutual border and my group will purchase the merchandise and assume all product ownership and liability after that transaction had been complete.

You may be wondering who I am and how I know about your operation. Feel free to conduct your own investigation into my identity, but I am afraid your efforts will be in vain. Like you, I protect my anonymity. That I know your identity should tell you how wide my influence is spread.

I know your product prices and I accept those terms, cash on delivery. My only terms are, for distribution in the United States, you deal with my organization exclusively.

Please consider this an initial proposal and tell Senor Victor Benitez my representative, Mr. Albert Smith, will contact him soon to arrange a meeting to answer your questions and fine tune our arrangement. If you are interested in pursuing this venture, please indicate that to Mr. Smith. This will be my final correspondence with you or your people. I suggest you destroy this letter after sharing it with Senor Benitez.

Sincerely Yours,
A Friend

Benitez rubbed his chin and looked quizzically across the table at his boss and asked, "What do you make of this?"

"I was going to ask you the same question. Go ahead and share it with Jorge," Vasquez replied and continued, "Do you have any idea who our "friend" might be?"

"I don't have a clue, but it smells like a set up. Who could be in such a position to know about you and our operation, and who could have his own distribution network already set up and be capable to handle our U.S. distribution and able to make such an outrageous proposal?" Benitez asked.

"I don't know, but it may be worth cautiously looking into. When this Mr. Smith contacts you, let me know the particulars of this proposed meeting. If we agree to meet, I must insist to know the identity of our new friend. If Mr. Smith is reluctant to tell you, I want you to persuade him, comprende?" Vasquez said with a tilt of his head.

A sly smile crossed Benitez's lips and he replied, "Comprende, Senor Vasquez."

The small drone aircraft hovered above the hot and dry Arizona desert at an altitude of five thousand feet. Its' small size and quiet battery powered motor made it undetectable from the ground. The only cargo it carried was a high resolution digital video camera with a zoom lens capable of detecting an ant crawling across the desert floor below.

Over a thousand mile from the craft, Sol Goldsmith, Sean O'Farrell, George Armstrong and Bernard Rusk sat in the Armstrong's den watching the scene being transmitted from the drone's video camera. Rusk held a joy stick control in his lap. Their eyes were riveted on a large screen television set. Rusk maneuvered the joy stick and the view on the screen panned in a three hundred and sixty degree sweep of the horizon.

"Right now we're looking at the small border town of Douglas, Arizona. It's about ten miles southwest of the meeting location," Rusk commented and continued, "As I recall, it's the same location where your team met with a cousin of Jesse Rivera and the Police Chief of Agua Pietà, Mexico.

He maneuvered the camera and followed State Highway Eighty out of Douglas heading northeast where it picked up two dark colored SUVs as they turned off the highway onto a sandy dirt road heading northeast.

He zoomed in on the two vehicles and said, "The lead car is holding four of Benitez's security men and Benitez and his driver are in the second SUV."

Moving the camera ahead of the two SUVs and down the dirt road several miles he stopped and backed the camera view out to reveal what appeared to be an old unused and broken down barn, corral and windmill. A silver SUV was parked on the far side of the corral and a table was set up and a man and a woman were sitting around it.

The two watched as the trailing SUV stopped several hundred yards from their location and the lead SUV approached slowly and parked. Four men, with machine pistols drawn, got out of the vehicle. From the front passenger seat emerged Jorge Bautista and after surveying the surroundings he motioned for two of his companions to search the barn and the other one to circle it.

He approached the couple at the table and smiling said, "You must be Mr. Smith. I'm sorry for the rude entrance, but Senor Benitez insists on taking every precaution."

"I understand Senor Bautista. Please take a seat and allow me to introduce my wife, Jane Smith," Jesse Leone said amiably.

Mary Dinosa smiled amiably and said, "It's nice to meet you Senor Bautista."

"It is my pleasure, Senora Smith, and I will sit in a moment," Bautista replied.

He walked over to the silver SUV and opened the rear door, inspected the interior and then turned toward his three men emerging from the barn and after receiving nods from them he turned toward the awaiting SUV and waved a come on. He took a seat at the table and the three men took up spaced positions about twenty feet behind him with their weapons at their sides.

Victor Benitez approached the table and said, "Ah, Mr. Smith, we finally meet."

After introductions were made, Jesse reached down toward an ice cooler at his side and noticing Bautista move his hand toward his waist band, he immediately raised his hands, palms out and said, "Oh sorry, I just thought a cold beer would be appreciated by all."

"That sounds good," Benitez said.

Jesse produced four Pacifico beers and passed them out. Dinosa declined and Jesse asked Benitez if his men would like one.

"No thank you, they are still working," he replied with a smile and then turning serious, he continued, "Mr. Smith, I'm sorry, but before we can begin any serious negotiations, my boss insists on knowing the identity of your boss and our new friend."

"I'm sorry too, but I cannot reveal his identity, but…" Jesse stopped abruptly when the four men standing behind Benitez and Bautista raised and locked and loaded their weapons.

"Like I said, Mr. Smith, I must insist on knowing your bosses name or I will have to terminate this meeting now," Benitez snarled menacingly.

"Geeeronimo!" Jesse yelled.

"What the…" Benitez started confused and stopped when he noticed a lump of sand and grass rise from the desert earth out of the corner of his eye not more than twenty feet from him. Two more lumps began to appear surrounding them and emerging from those lumps were three very ugly desert creatures with AR16s aimed at him. He heard a tapping noise and looked down. Across from him, underneath her purse bag, he was looking at the muzzle of a forty-five hand gun that Dinosa had aimed right at his midsection.

Jesse looked at Bautista and smiling said, "I too am sorry, but I also take every precaution," and looking back at Benitez added, "Let's not make this spoil our little chat, shall we?"

Watching this scene a thousand miles away, the group gathered in Armstrong's den let out a collective sigh of relief.

"I mean, we are here to discuss a mutually financially rewarding proposition, are we not?" Jesse continued unaffected, "and I was about to explain that our friend will reveal himself to Senor Vasquez when the time is right."

"Okay, what specifically is your proposal?" Benitez gruffly asked.

"First, in a spirit of trust and cooperation and just in case one of our security people should accidently discharge their weapon, why don't we at least allow them to lower their weapons?" Jesse said calmly.

Benitez nodded at his men and they lowered their guns and Jesse's team followed suit.

"Ah, that's much better. Now, we are prepared to take delivery of as much product as you can deliver provided the girls are young and relatively good looking. We know your price before the unfortunate disruption was between ten and fifteen thousand U.S. dollars. We are prepared to offer you twenty thousand dollars per unit with the right to refuse merchandise we determine to be unusable. We will take delivery at a location of your choice as long as it is at or near a border town on your side and we will pay with cash at that time. We have only two major stipulations if we both agree to enter this business relationship," Jesse said.

"So what are these stipulations?" Benitez queried, tilting his head.

"First, we insist that you do not do business with anyone else within the U.S. or Canada. We require an exclusive franchise for these two countries. Second, once we have paid for and taken possession of the merchandise, it will be our sole responsibility and business to transport it across the border. My boss will tolerate no interference on either side of the border from your organization nor will we ask for your support once we take possession.

"We anticipate a friendly business association as long as we respect each other's position, but as you can see," Jesse said looking around at his desert creatures, "my boss will not tolerate nor anticipate any more scenes like this one today. If that should happen again, you can consider our business relationship severed with consequences. Understand, our friend has friends in very high places."

"Is that all?" Benitez asked.

"That's about it amigo. Take this information back to your boss and we'd appreciate a quick response so, if necessary, we can pursue other opportunities. If Senor Vasquez should decide not to accept our offer, we will take no offense and part ways amiably,"

"I will do that," Benitez said and after glancing at Dinosa and looking back at Jesse, he added with a wink, "Mr. Smith, I like your style."

He rose and nodded to his men who retreated to their vehicles and sped off. When they were well out of sight, Ian, Grant and Gary Brown laid their weapons on the table and began peeling off their camouflaged nets, revealing their identities.

Brown looked to the skies and waved. Back in Armstrong's den, Solomon Goldsmith said surprised, "That looks like Gary Brown."

Rusk smiled and said, "It is. He expressed to me that he really wanted to see this through and I agreed he'd earned that right. In fact, he also indicated he might want to resign from the CIA after this mission. It looks like you fellows might be adding another member to your team."

Benitez was escorted out onto the Veranda at Hacienda de la Vasquez by the same large burly man he had come to know simply as Pedro. He joined Senor Vasquez and sat down at the patio table.

"How did the meeting go and who is this mysterious new friend of ours?" Vasquez asked, puffing on a slim cigar.

For the next half an hour, Benitez spared no detail in explaining the events surrounding the meeting and when he was done Vasquez said accusingly, "It sounds like you underestimated this Mister Smith and had a piss poor plan."

"You may be right, Senor Vasquez," Benitez replied with a shrug and then continued, "My men thought they had cleared the area and so did I. I admit, I did not anticipate the senorita with the hand gun, and it was uncanny how well camouflaged his three amigos were. They were no more than twenty or thirty feet from me when they showed themselves. I'm almost sure these people are ex-military."

"What do you think of their proposal? Do you think these people are legitimate?" Vasquez queried.

"Ah," Benitez started hesitantly, "We have never heard of these people before, but that might be a good thing. If we have not heard of them then I doubt the authorities have either."

"What if they are the authorities?" Vasquez proposed.

"I think we should have Jorge deliver a small shipment, as a test. I will observe from a distance and we can follow where they transport the girls and how they get them across the border," Benitez said and added, "That should tell us something about their legitimacy and I might remind you, we have a massive traffic jam at the border right now."

"Go ahead and do it, but Victor, be careful my friend."

―

The ranch style sprawling home sat nestled in a grove of willow and maple trees in the middle of a hundred acres of sugar beet field just five miles north east of Douglas, Arizona, a town that shared the border with Agua Prieta. Grant was tending to steaks on the barbeque on the outside patio while Ian and Mary were preparing a tossed green salad and baked beans just inside the patio entrance in the kitchen. Jesse and Brown were lounging about at a deck table next to the swimming pool engaged in a game of cribbage.

Everyone stopped what they were doing when they spied a dust trail following a red compact pick-up truck coming from the highway down the quarter mile long driveway leading to the house.

From the sliding glass door and holding an AR-16 rifle, Ian yelled, "Everybody take your positions!"

Grant grabbed his weapon and squatted behind the brick barbeque pit with a clear view of the driveway at the front of the garage, while Brown sprinted to the corner at the rear of the garage and Jesse took up a position at the corner of the home. With a 45 caliber semi-automatic pistol tucked in her belt beneath her apron and Ian behind her with his hand gun tucked in the small of his back, the pair walked toward the front of the garage toward the approaching truck.

When the truck stopped the door opened and a petite, pixie-like woman jumped out from the driver's side door and yelled, "Hey Mary, thought I'd join you!"

She was wearing mid-thigh length denim shorts, a safari shirt and hiking boots. She had changed the color of her hair from blonde to a more natural brunette look.

Ian broke into a broad grin and Dinosa shrieked, "Joan, what the hell are you doing here?" as she ran out to greet her.

She nearly bowled Richards over as she met her with a hug and Richards responded with, "Jesus Christ Mary, it's good to see you too. A little birdie told me where I could find you and while taking a little vacation after I tied up some loose ends in Detroit, I decided to join you. You didn't think I'd let you do this without me, did you?"

"It's great to have you here," Dinosa said and turning towards Grant she yelled, "Put on another steak Grant!"

After supper, Jesse and Grant were in the living room in front of the television watching a Giant versus Dodger baseball game when Grant roared out, "Yeah, that's what I'm talkn' 'bout!"

"Ah shit, he's a lucky has been," Jesse moaned.

"Yeah, well that lucky has been just struck out the Dodger's three best hitters in a row," Grant chuckled.

On the patio just outside sitting around the patio table, Mary looked across at Joan and asked, "So, how did it go in Detroit?"

"Oh, you guys should have been there. It was perfect. Alderman Franks was attending a fund raiser dinner to announce his candidacy for Mayor. He had just finished speaking to the room full of Detroit's most elite bragging about how, under his watch, the violent crime and homicide rate in his district was down ten percent from last year when we approached him and as I slapped the cuffs on him I said in my loudest voice, "Jamal Franks, you are under arrest on Rico charges for ongoing criminal activities and, among other things, for conspiring to transport underage girls across state lines for the purpose of sexual exploitation.

"I thought he'd shit himself. The look on his face was priceless and the entire city saw it on the eleven o'clock news."

Ian lifted his glass of wine and said, "I propose a toast to Joan and Mary. Their efforts have led to effectively shutting down two of our nation's largest criminal activity rings."

"Hear, hear," Brown said lifting his glass, "and to the Director of the FBI who is bragging about bringing an end to illegal sex trafficking in the country."

The celebration was interrupted when Jesse, standing at the patio door holding a ringing cell phone said, "Its Benitez."

Everyone went silent as he answered the phone, "Good evening Senor Benitez."

After several minutes of conversation, Jesse ended it by saying, "That sounds good. I'll get back to you in a few minutes."

Everyone gathered in the living room and Grant hit the mute button on the television.

"That was quick. What did he have to say?" Ian asked.

"He wants a transaction to go down tomorrow night and since he thought we'd still be in the area, he suggested it happen in Agua Prieta. It'll be at a broken down abandoned house just south of town. I'm familiar with the area. He indicated he has ten girls to sell us. I got the feeling this is some sort of test, like can we get the cash and move that fast," Jesse replied.

Ian thought for a moment and then said, "Call him back and tell him it's a go. I'll arrange for the money to be wired first thing in the morning. Then I need you to put me in contact with your cousin and also your friend the local sheriff."

Jesse Leone was born and raised in Douglas and was a friend of Joe Jimenez in high school.

Jimenez was a Cochise County Deputy Sheriff, the son of the late Sheriff Edwardo Jimenez who was assassinated several years ago by 'El Diablo', the Mexican drug cartel. At that time Jesse and Joe reunited when the Justice Foundation team needed local help on a mission to break up the drug cartel. Joe introduced the team to the then interim and now elected Cochise County Sheriff Billy Burnett and the two proved to be essential allies.

Another local law enforcement connection he had was an older cousin, Maria Hernandez, who was Agua Prieta's Chief of Police and had also helped the team with information and tactical support.

The following afternoon, Jesse and Dinosa pulled up in front of the abandoned house in a run downed area just south of Agua Prieta and parked behind a dark colored SUV. They strolled up to the front door and knocked. Dinosa was carrying two brief cases. The door was opened by a large Latino man who invited the couple in and then frisked them. Standing on the other side of the room was Victor Benitez who said almost apologetically, "Sorry for the precautionary measures."

"Understood, but I believe we will come to trust one another," Jesse simply replied.

Benitez nodded at the large man who walked to an adjoining bedroom door and opened it and gruffly ordered, "Rapido."

Ten young girls filed into the room in various manners of dress, all with their heads down in a posture of resignation. Dinosa guessed they ranged in age from twelve to eighteen years old as she inspected each girl by raising their chins and looking into their eyes as she went from girl to girl. She found it very difficult to restrain her emotions of pity and rage, but after inspecting the last girl she turned and nodded her approval to Jesse.

Picking up the larger brief case he handed it to Benitez and said, "It appears we have a deal. There's two hundred thousand American dollars in this."

Benitez, in turn, handed the valise to his partner who opened it and began counting the money. As the man picked out stacks of one hundred dollars bills wrapped and marked in ten thousand dollar increments, Benitez asked, "How are you going to transport the girl across the border?"

"That my friend is none of your business, but I will tell you as soon as I make a call, a local school bus escorted by an Agua Prieta police cruiser will pull up outside. I suggest, if you are uncomfortable with law officials, you and your friend should probably leave now," Jesse replied.

Benitez snickered and said, "We're in no hurry."

Jesse tilted his head and said, "That's up to you."

"It's all here, Senor Benitez," the large man interrupted.

Jesse retrieved a cell phone from his pocket, dialed a number and simply said, "It's good."

A moment later a police cruiser pulled up out front followed by a yellow school bus marked, 'Publico Escuela Secondaria de Agua Prieta'.

"Our ride is here," Jesse remarked, and as Dinosa began escorting the girls outside, he picked up the smaller brief case and handing it to Benitez, added, "This is another fifty thousand dollars. A show our good faith. Hope to hear from you again."

—

"Senor Vasquez, I must say these gringos are strange, but the transaction went off like, how do they say, clock work," Benitez reported from his cell phone.

He explained how it went down and that Jorge Bautista and several of his men followed the caravan across the border into Douglas, Arizona. "It was amazing, they were simply waved through on the Americano side," he said incredulously and added, "These people must have some kind of connections."

"Or they're federal agents," Arturo Vasquez commented on the other end of the line.

"I don't think so. They knew we were following them. Bautista followed them to a ranch home north of Douglas and when they pulled up to the driveway a Sheriff's vehicle stopped them and the Cochise

County Sheriff himself strongly suggested they return to Mexico and mind their own business. It seems so bazaar."

"I will leave it up to you, Victor. Arrange for future transactions at your discretion and also find out where they are shipping these girls," Vasquez ordered.

—

Following their brief encounter with Jorge Bautista and his men, Sheriff Joe Jimenez and his Deputy Billy Barnett continued down the driveway to the ranch house and pulled up behind the bus just as Dinosa followed the last girl into the home.

The girls were greeted by Sister Elana, a young Nun the team had flown in that morning from St. Leo's Sanctuary House in San Jose, California. She was upbeat as she warmly welcomed each girl and asked what their names were. Speaking in perfect Spanish, she told them they were safe now and they soon would be allowed to shower after filling out a simple questionnaire that required their full names, the country and city of their origin and family contact information. If they could not write or read, she would be happy to translate.

Sheriff Jimenez and Billy Barnett entered the room and approached Ian who was standing in a corner of the room with Dinosa and Joan Richards.

After thanking them, Ian made introductions.

"What's with the first letter of your first and last names being the same? Is that a Texas male thing? I mean, should I call you Jay Jay and Dee Dee?" Dinosa asked goofily.

When the two men looked queerly at her, Ian shook his head and smiling said, "Don't mind her. We believe she's mentally challenged."

"Is there anything else we can do?" Jimenez asked as Dinosa reddened.

"You've done enough and thanks again," Ian replied.

As they turned to leave, Barnett tipped his cowboy hat brim at Dinosa and with a wide grin said, "Vios con diaz, Senorita Locco."

When his back was turned, Dinosa tugged on Ian's shirt sleeve and whispered, "What did he say to me?"

Richards tried to stifle a laugh and failed as Ian simply chuckled, "Never mind, he just called you a crazy lady."

Most of the girls were showing the beginning signs of life and optimism. Some were even speaking and giggling with each other. Not wanting to break the growing joyous atmosphere, Dinosa good naturedly replied, waving her index finger at Ian, "Well, he's right and don't you forget it."

After the girls had showered and changed into fresh clean clothes Sister Elana had brought with her, they feasted on a traditional Mexican meal prepared by Jesse Ramirez and then the group gathered around the open fire pit on the back yard lawn. Sister Elana retrieved a guitar and the group sang along as she played music from their native lands.

The team was on the patio watching the girls and drinking various libations.

"Kind of warms and breaks your heart all at the same time, doesn't it?" Grant commented and then looking at Richards asked, "Where will they go from here?"

"Well, thanks to the charity of George Armstrong, tomorrow morning Sister Elana will escort them by bus to Phoenix where they'll fly on Mr. Armstrong's corporate jet back to San Jose, California and the girl's center at Saint Leo's Sanctuary House. Their needs will be well taken care of, believe me," Richards replied.

Later that night, Dinosa stepped out of the shower, toweled off, hair-dried her shoulder length brunette locks and walked into the adjoining bedroom with the towel wrapped around her. Ian was sitting up in bed with the table light on, a note pad on his lap and talking on the telephone.

"That sounds good and thanks, I'll talk to you in the morning," Ian said, hanging up the phone.

"Who was that?" Dinosa queried.

"It was Bernie Rusk. He just wanted to know how it went today and also informed me Senor Arturo Vasquez will be attending an international trade show in Chicago later this month and that may be the opportune time to reveal myself as his 'friend'. Old Bernie is an amazing guy."

Slipping off her towel and crawling into bed, Dinosa propped herself up on one elbow said, "You know, speaking of amazing people, I visited the Saint Leo's Sanctuary House with Joan, and those people are very amazing."

She waited for a nod of acknowledgement and continued, "Don't you think they would be a great cause for your foundation?"

"Now that you mentioned it, the board has discussed the possibility of just such a proposal, along with several other similar institutes around the country. We plan on creating a separate fund for that purpose, but we need someone to administer it. Would you be interested?"

Dinosa reached up and grabbed Ian around the neck and gruffly pulled him on top of her, the note pad falling harmlessly to the floor.

"Come here, you big hunk of woman bait, you," she giggled.

They made love, serenaded by the young girl's voices coming from the back yard, "Sol, sol, solcato caliente un poquito…"

CHAPTER THIRTEEN

Valerie Kane knocked on the door of the suite located on the twenty-fifth floor of the Mark Hopkins Hotel and was greeted by Bernard Rusk. They embraced one another and Rusk said, "Ah Valerie, it's so good to see you again. Come in."

"It's good to see you too, Professor Rusk," Kane said as she entered the room and Rusk took her coat and hung it in the entrance closet.

Rusk turned around and grasping her arm and escorting her into the front room he commented, "Wow, it's been a long time since anyone addressed me as Professor, but I did peg you as one of my students who would excel in life. What can I get you?"

"A glass of red wine would be nice," she replied.

"Sounds good, please, take a seat," Rusk said, indicating the couch as he walked up the three steps of the split level room to the wet bar and uncorked a bottle of wine.

Kane sat down on the sofa and noticed three file boxes placed in a row on the coffee table in front of her. She realized this was not going to be a social meeting and the boxes perked her curiosity. She resisted the urge to peek into the covered boxes.

Rusk returned with a bottle of wine and two glasses, poured the wine and handed a glass to Valerie and sat down on the easy chair opposite her and started, "Val, I'm sure by now you know I'm more than an analyst for the CIA. I don't really know what my official title should be, but I consider myself a loyal American citizen and I have a favor to ask of you."

"Come on Bernie, we didn't call you Professor 'Los Santos' in law school for nothing and I wasn't born yesterday, so please continue."

"Okay, I'll get right to the point. These boxes in front of you contain reports and findings of an extensive investigation into criminal activity of several key political figures. Most of the data was compiled by Doctor and Mrs. Tanaka at my request. I must say that Belinda's nickname 'Snoopy' applies equally to the both of them.

"Because I work for the CIA, it would be inappropriate for me to turn this information over to the FBI, but because the Tanaka's have consulted with your department in the past, it would certainly be reasonable to accept that this is a San Francisco District Attorney investigation and you could present it to the feds."

Kane tilted her head and with a pert smile retorted, "Let me get this straight. You're asking me, to perjure myself to a federal agency and tell them my office is responsible for gathering this information. I would set myself and my office up for a war against several key politicians. Pray tell, why would I want to do this?"

"Perhaps, because you are also a loyal American citizen. Listen Val, I don't expect an answer now. Please, take the boxes and review them. They contain irrefutable evidence that a U.S. Senator and a senior California State Senator have been receiving campaign contributions and other personal perks from foreign sources, one of which is responsible for the dead Asian girls that washed up on your shores.

"There's certainly no harm in at least reading this material and I'm fairly certain after you have, you'll share it with the FBI," Rusk concluded.

Kane sat back, crossed her legs, looked up at the ceiling exasperated and cried, "Bernard Rusk, you son of a bitch, you're blackmailing me! We should have called you 'El Diablo'."

Rusk simply smiled and nodded.

—

Ralph Schwartz was a small man, but he compensated for his slight physical stature with his cunning intelligence. He prided himself with his ability to be at least one step ahead of the next fellow. He approached life as if it were a chess game and he possessed that uncanny ability to maintain the upper hand by always anticipating his opponents moves, sometimes two or three moves in advance. He never lost a game and always captured his opponent's king.

He had been taught well by his father, a German staff officer with the Nazi S.S. in World War II who immigrated to the United States after the war and stealthily managed to avoid detection and prosecution for his war crimes and raise a respectable family. On his deathbed his father revealed his past to his son and told him how proud he was of him and that he must never tell a soul. Even his mother did not know and he admonished his son he must sometimes be ruthless in pursuit of the prize.

He listened to his father and graduated at the top of his class with a degree in political science from the University of California at Berkeley and then went on to earn his MBA in business administration. He realized that good back room politics yielded more power to the helmsman who steered the rudder than the politician himself and even as a student he involved himself in local elections as a campaign fund raising manager and political organizer. He earned a reputation of being an effective behind the scenes political promoter and he eventually cemented his worth by leading the successful campaign for a huge underdog candidate against a well-entrenched and incumbent U.S. Senator for the party's nomination. He was crowned Chief of Staff for the newly elected Senator from California, John Quincy Abrams.

Senator Abrams was now in his third term and a leader in his party. Despite the party's almost devastating collapse following the disgraceful fall from grace and eventual resignation of then President Barrymore Benjamin several years ago, the Senator and his Chief of Staff aimed their sights at the nation's highest office.

Ralph Schwartz knew he was responsible for his boss' successes. He had managed to keep his boss protected during the Benjamin fiasco and scandal with cunning backroom deals, coercion and outright extortion. He sat now in his office separated by a conference room from Senator Abram's office pondering how it had all come full circle. He wondered how it had happened but more important, he was attempting to develop a plan that would allow him to escape with the least amount of personal harm.

But, how can I mount a defense when I don't even know who my enemy is, he asked himself? His accuser didn't even identify himself or the agency he worked for. He had exhausted every means at his disposal, and they were vast, to identify this person to no avail.

His thoughts were interrupted by his secretary on the intercom, "Sir, it's a Valerie Kane for you on line one."

"Who?" he asked, confused.

"Valerie Kane, she's the San Francisco District Attorney. She told me to tell you it concerns a man named Vasquez and added you'd want to talk to her. Shall I tell her you're unavailable?"

"Ah, ah no, I'll take the call," he replied trying to compose himself.

A moment later he cleared his voice and answered the phone calmly, "Hello Ms. Kane, how can I help you?"

"Well," Kane began, "I've been reviewing the material you provided my investigator and I think you know how you can help me."

Schwartz's eyes widened and bulged with anger, "What, this is your investigation? The shit hole S.F. DA's office? Your investigator didn't even identify himself! This is bloody blackmail! It'll never hold up in a court of law!" he cried.

"We will find out, won't we?" Kane replied and added, "In the words of Shakespeare, Mr. Schwartz, even Hamlet had to admit he was hoisted by his own petard."

"But, your investigator promised I'd get total immunity if I cooperated," Schwartz pleaded in protest.

"My investigator has no such authority, but he does have the authority to lie while conducting an investigation," Kane stated flatly.

"You son of a bitch, you whore, you'll never get away with this!" he cried.

"I can assure you Mr. Schwartz, I am no woman's son, but before I turn this investigation over to the Department of Justice and the FBI, I have one more task for you," Kane replied calmly.

That's it, my out card, Schwartz mind was spinning. He knew the Attorney General and the man owed him plenty. He would play that card when the time was right. An aura of bliss and self-confidence suddenly encompassed him as he realized he was once again in control and would win this game.

In a civil tone he said, "Of course Ms. Kane, what is it you'd have me to do?"

"I want you to wire yourself with a bug, I know you know how to do that. Then I want you to get your boss to admit he knows Senor Vasquez and about the illegal campaign contributions that Vasquez has been funneling into that account. I also want him to acknowledge he is aware of why his wife drives a new Mercedes Benz and his son drives a brand new Corvette and who donated over one million dollars to his stock portfolio. You will also get him to say he knows about Senor Vasquez's illegal human sex slave trafficking and gun running activities and I want all of this on tape.

"Oh, I almost forgot. I need him to say that all of these gifts were in exchange for you passing on secret information you received from the Senator as a result of his position on all of the Federal Law Enforcement oversight committees. Do you think you can do that?"

"I can handle that," Schwartz lied, knowing he had the ace up his sleeve, but as an after-thought he added, "I have only two questions. One; don't you think he'll get a little suspicious if I go marching into his office and confront him with all these questions? And two; if I am successful, what do I get in return?"

"Let me worry about when you need to be wired. You only need to have the bug ready when I give you a call. At that time, all you need to know is that he will volunteer most of the information I need. As far as your reward is concerned; I know you are personal friends with our Attorney General and you can work out a deal with him.

"You should also know, this conversation is being taped, and it will mysteriously get released to the media should you fail. Do you still believe you can do this?" Kane stifled a chuckle.

"You fucking whore!"

Kane hung up the speaker phone and looked across her desk at Bernard Rusk and asked, "You think that worked?"

"That was perfect, my dear, and I hope it has not been too much trouble," he replied.

"You know, Professor, it is times like this that I'm glad you're on our side."

"You guys have been kept pretty busy. We've received three shipments totaling over fifty girls in less than a week," Rusk said into his cell phone.

"Yeah there seems to be an endless supply and apparently Vasquez is comfortable with our present arrangement and means of exchange," Ian replied from the ranch house outside the town of Douglas.

"Well, we've devised a plan that will curtail that endless supply, but it will require you to split up the team," Rusk said.

"Let's hear it," Ian remarked.

"Oooh, Antonio, I know this great little whore house in downtown Belize. The girls there will do anything for you for just a few pesos. After we drop off our cargo, I will take you there," the paunch bellied Guatemalan man said to his companion as they drove the cattle truck down the two lane pothole riddled road known as the Western Highway that started in Guatemala City and ended in Belize City on the Gulf of Mexico. Jungle forest lined both side of the highway.

"After we get paid, we can hire every whore in the city," cackled his ugly partner revealing only a half compliment of his original set of teeth.

As they rounded a corner they came upon a military styled jeep blocking their lane and two men in army dress standing beside it. They both had automatic weapons slung over their shoulders and one was holding a sign that read 'Alto'.

"What is this?" the ugly man exclaimed.

"Not to worry, Antonio," the driver said, patting the piece of paper in his breast pocket.

When they came to a stop, the man holding the sign laid it down, unslung his rifle to a present arms stance and stood in front of the truck's cab. The other man approached the driver's side window and said in Spanish, "What is your cargo?"

"It is cattle we are transporting to the port at Belize City, Senor," the man replied, handing him the folded piece of paper.

After reading the letter, Gary Brown took a step back and unslinging and leveling his rifle he ordered, "Both of you out of the truck. We will have to inspect your cargo."

"But Senor, the letter is from your superior officer, Colonel Montez," the man protested.

"I said out of the truck and I won't repeat it," Brown threatened.

The two men were directed to the side of the road and ordered to stay on their knees with their hands interlocked on top of their heads. Brown turned around and indicated to a waiting passenger car to proceed. Grant Wilson stood guard and Brown waved a come on toward the trees as he walked toward the rear of the truck.

Joan Richards emerged from the brush and met him at the tail gate. He unlatched and swung open the door. Nine young women and girls huddled shivering together near the front of the trailer.

Richards climbed up into the trailer and in her most comforting and cajoling voice said in Spanish, "It's all right girls. We're here to help you and no harm will come to you from now on."

She approached what she thought looked like the oldest girl, held out her hand and with pleading eyes said, "Please, come with us and we will take you to safety."

The frightened young woman slowly took her hand and Richards wrapped her in her arms and cried, "It will be okay, I promise."

She escorted her to the rear of the trailer and handed her off to Brown who helped her down followed by the rest of the girls.

"Okay, get them to the chopper and we'll be along shortly," he told Richards.

She led the girls back into the bush and through the jungle about a hundred yards where a helicopter awaited them in a clearing. The pilot started the engine as soon as he spotted them. The sound of the rotors blocked out the sound of two men screaming and two gun retorts. Several minutes later Brown and Grant emerged from the jungle and hopped aboard the chopper. Brown yelled at the pilot, "Let's get the hell out of here!"

As the craft rose, Richards asked with a yell above the engine sound, "What happened to the two men?"

"It's best if you don't know!" Brown yelled back as the chopper rose and swung around heading west just above the tree tops.

The following day, virtually every newspaper in Central and South America and every televised newscast reported the unseemly deaths of two Guatemalan men, alleged human sex slave traffickers, and published pictures of the two men strapped to trees, shot to death, standing with their pants down around their ankles and their severed penis' stuffed in their mouths. It was also reported, a note pinned to one of the victim's chest read;

Beware; this is what will happen to anyone who deals in the sex trafficking of our young girls and our daughters. We know who you are and we will find you and your fate will be the same as these two pigs.

The news spread north and by the following day in America it became the main topic of conversation and reporting on radio talk shows, cable news television and the nightly network news. Most of the American daily newspapers headlined the story and ran related articles. Overnight the plight of the victims of the international sex slave trafficking business became a sensation. Statistics and stories like the Asian girls who washed up on the beaches of San Francisco became international news.

Vigilante groups sprung up all over countries in Latin and South America and similar incidents of violence against known sex traders were being reported, forcing some countries to declare war on the illicit business.

The United Nation's Council on Human Rights introduced a resolution to establish this atrocity as an international crime and, with the exception of several abstaining Mideast countries, it was passed by the General Assembly without a single dissenting vote. Leaders of Women's Rights groups and politicians lined up for interviews on television talk shows.

Valerie Kane and Bernard Rusk sat in her living room watching the television and enjoying a snifter of fine brandy. The screen flashed to a distinguished looking, middle aged woman sitting behind a counter top inside a news studio next to a stately looking wavy gray-haired gentleman.

"Good evening everybody, I'm Janis Costas and your about to witness 'Behind the News'. I'd like to introduce my very special guest tonight, the Honorable Senior Senator from California, John Quincy Abrams. Welcome to the program Senator Abrams."

The senator smiled brightly and said, "It's my pleasure to be here and thank you for inviting me."

Sitting in the green room adjacent to the studio and watching the newscast on a monitor, Ralph Schwartz bent over in his chair, put his elbows on his knees, covered his face with his hands and whispered a moan, "Ah, Jesus, you fucking idiot."

"I'd like for you, Senator, and my audience to watch the following news clip and get your reaction," Costas said.

The screen turned to a scene of men in hazmat suits lifting the bodies of soaking wet bloated Asian girls from the sand and the camera following them as they trudged up the beach to a waiting van where the stretchers were placed. Sad, melodramatic violin music accompanied the scene.

The screen shifted back to a close up of Costas with her hand placed over her mouth and an expression of astonished sadness in her eyes. After composing herself she commented.

"Wow, that's a tough scene to watch."

She then asked;

"As the Senator from the state where just several weeks ago this footage was shot and as many as a dozen young Asian girls were discovered drowned and washed up on a beach in San Francisco and traced to being victims of the sex slave industry, what is your reaction to the now international outcry against those who are perpetuating and profiting from such crimes?"

"In a word, Janis, I'm appalled. As you know I have a record in the Senate as being a staunch supporter of women's rights and I've written and introduced bills that would help bring an end to the atrocities we just witnessed," he replied sternly.

Costas followed up and asked, "And what would those bills be Senator, exactly?"

Abrams cleared his throat and uttered, "Well, for one the equal work…I mean equal pay for equal work act."

"Oh my God!" Kane screamed at the television, "He can't really believe that equal pay for equal work will help end the sex slave business!" and turning towards Rusk asked, "Is it time I make that phone call to Schwartz?"

"Not yet, Val, but soon," Rusk replied.

In the studio green room Schwartz couldn't contain himself and screamed, "You fucking, fucking idiot!"

A young female assistant producer stuck her head inside the green room door and asked, "Is everything okay, Mr. Schwartz?"

Costas just shook her head looking incredulous and then asked, "How do you respond to the photographs and stories surrounding the apparent murder of the two Guatemalan men several days ago and stories now coming out of Mexico and Central and South America of vigilante groups hunting down and slaying suspected sex slave traders?"

"Well, as a politician and law abiding citizen, I have to condemn these actions, but as the father of two beautiful daughters and the grandfather of three little girls, I can't say I wouldn't do the same thing to protect them," he replied turning his head and looking directly into the camera.

"God, I'd give anything to be the prosecuting attorney at his trial. Can you imagine the reaction from the jury after I played that last clip to them during closing arguments? I'd stop it and play back, 'I can't say I wouldn't do the same thing to protect them'," Kane beamed.

"It might be a little overkill, no pun intended, if you added, 'Now in this country we can't cut off his dick and leave him choking on it, but…'" Rusk chuckled.

Kane began laughing almost hysterically, before she calmed down and red faced said, "I'm sorry. This is not a laughing matter, although I find that image very humorous."

A sober look came over her and after turning off the broadcast, she asked seriously, "Bernie, do you think all of this will make a difference?"

"That's a good question and I wish I could give you a concrete answer. I do believe if this issue remains relevant and the world media keeps it that way, it will go a long way to stemming it. I have never seen such international outrage. Even the Russians and Chinese are cracking down on human trafficking, but I'm afraid to say where it is abused the most and the demand is the highest is in the Middle East where some of the rich Sultanates, Emirs and their families and associates have an insatiable appetite for this debauchery. Unfortunately, the irony of that is, it is helping to finance the very terrorist organizations that wish to overthrow them.

"You know, I'm not a very religious man, but I do believe that in the end good will prevail over evil. In the words of Albert Einstein; 'When there is no good and only evil exists, there can be no life'.

"May I use your phone?" he asked.

Kane nodded and pointed at a cordless phone on the coffee table in front of them.

Rusk picked it up and dialed, "Hey Ian, how's it going?"

"We're doing fine. What's on your mind?"

"I'm on my way to Chicago and I'd like you to join me tomorrow. I'm staying at the McCormick Place Hotel. It's time to begin plan B."

"We'll be there with bells on," Ian said hanging up.

—

Dinosa pulled the mini bus up to the front of the 'Sisters of Mary House' on Alamo Boulevard in San Antonio, Texas, and looked over with a smile at Richards and said, "Well, we made it."

The nine girls in the back were crowded up to the window facing the Cathedral that was attached to a sprawling two story structure. They were all wide eyed and whispering and giggling.

Richards turned in her seat and in Spanish said, "Girls, we have arrived and you're looking at our new home for a while," and opening the side door she added, "Now, follow me."

They filed out of the bus trailed by Dinosa and as they approached a double door to the building marked 'Entrance', and before Richards could knock, the doors were opened and two Nuns dressed in modern habits greeted them. The shorter one stepped out and hugging Richards, exclaimed, "Oh Joan, it's so good to see you again."

Richards returned the greeting and introduced Dinosa and then turning toward the group of girls she announced, "And these are the lovely young girls I was telling you about."

"Oh girls," the Nun spoke in Spanish, "Come in, come in and welcome, we've been waiting for you."

She escorted the group across the foyer and down a hall to another set of double doors labeled 'Auditorium/Gymnasium' and opened both doors. They were greeted by applause from over a hundred other young women and girls standing in formation dressed in traditional parochial white blouses and pleated skirts.

The young girl Richards had first approached in the front of the cattle car turned and holding both of Joan's hand and with a tear in her eye said, "Gracias, Senorita Joan, mucho gracias."

—

PART III
Justice

'Human progress is neither automatic nor inevitable...Every step toward the goal of justice requires sacrifice, suffering and struggle; the tireless exertions and passionate concerns of dedicated Individuals.' Martin Luther King, Jr.

CHAPTER FOURTEEN

Gary Brown and Grant Wilson, with an arm draped over each other's shoulders, weaved and stumbled as they started up the stairway carved out of the old lava cliff that switch backed and led up from the beach to a cliff top home some two hundred feet above. It was located about five miles south of Rosarito, Mexico and was the residence of Jorge Batista, leader of the ruthless Mexican cartel known as 'El Diablo'.

The two were dressed in shabby cutoffs and soiled tee shirts and were bare footed. Brown was singing loudly and off key the tune 'La Bamba' and Grant pretended to mumble along. In his free hand, Brown held a brown paper bag and as they spotted a large Latino man holding a rifle and approaching from above, he stopped and pretended to take a swig from the silencer attached to a nine millimeter pistol that was concealed in the bag.

"Halt!" he large man ordered and continued in Spanish, "This is a private access and you are not permitted to use it. Did you not see the posted sign at the bottom?"

Brown looked up and acting surprised and through squinted eyes he slurred in Spanish, "Oh Senor, we are so sorry. We are just trying to get to my car."

He release his arm from around Grant and pointing the bag at the large man he said, "Here amigo, have a drink."

The man was about to reply when a loud 'plink' was heard and a red hole appeared on the man's forehead just between his eyes and he tumbled forward landing at the pair's feet. They dragged the dead body to the side of the stair case and shoved him off and down into the darkness.

Brown feigned a look of amazement at the bag he was holding and tilting his head he whispered, "Damn, I didn't realize what a wallop this Mexican Tequila packs."

"Okay," Grant began in a whisper, "Our intelligence says the home is guarded by one man at the rear," he pointed with his thumb down the cliff and shrugged, "and a man out front. Other than Jorge and his female companionship, there should be only one guard in the home manning the surveillance monitors. Hopefully, when we disarm the camera covering the rear entrance and he's unable to raise his buddy he'll come to investigate. And, of course, we have to hope Jorge didn't invite a bunch of his gang banger buddies to a sleep over and we have to shoot our way out. "

Brown nodded his approval and the two continued up the flight of stairs until they were several steps below the landing and veranda of the split level home. Brown nudged Grant and pointed at a compact camera mounted above and aimed at the outside sliding glass entrance to the residence. Grant climbed over the railing and supporting himself on the corner of the step and holding himself with his right hand on the top rail, he reached up with his other hand and grasped the lowest bar of the veranda railing. In one motion he released his right hand, swung out into open space and reached up and grasped the veranda railing with his right hand. Dangling over the rocks and beach below, he maneuvered himself away from the stair case until he reached a point where he would be out of range of the camera and lifted himself up, scaled the railing and onto the porch that ran the length of the back of the home.

Watching with admiration as his new very large friend effortlessly complete this stunt, he wondered if he were still in good enough shape to have accomplished it. He vowed to himself he would start working out again.

Once on the veranda, Grant produced a ski mask from his rear pocket, put it on, covering his face, and retrieved his hand gun from the small of his back. He crept across the porch approaching the camera from the rear and reached up and pointed the camera up toward the eaves.

Brown, slipping on a ski mask, sprinted up the final few steps and ran to the far corner of the veranda and took up a shooting position on one knee. Grant squatted down behind a lounge chair on the other side of the entrance, his gun pointed in that direction.

Several minutes later a light came on just inside the glass door and a small man dressed in a bright orange sweat suit approached the door, opened it and as he stepped out onto the veranda, said, "Hernando, where the fuck…"

Two 'plinks' rang out almost simultaneous and the bright orange sweat suit twisted and fell to the deck of the porch. Brown and Grant ran from their cover and leapt over the dead man and entered the home. They were in a large open room that appeared to be a den with easy chairs and a sofa facing a large screen television mounted on the far wall to their right and a wet bar and tables situated on the other side of the room. A hallway on the opposite wall led to the front of the residence. A stairway to its right led up to a landing and a bedroom and office on the second story.

They crept up the staircase and when they reached the landing, Brown stood guard with his hand gun at the ready as Grant proceeded to the bedroom door. He opened it and stepping in, he switched on the light. The three occupants in the bed remained asleep and Grant yelled, "Hey!"

Jorge Batista managed to lift himself onto one elbow and squint through sleeping eyes at the figure standing at the foot of his bed. The last thing he would ever hear was Grant saying, "Adios."

Batista's head jerked back and a splatter of blood, bone and brain matter exploded out of the back of his skull and besmirched the headboard behind him. He was flanked in his death bed on one side by a shivering blond and bare breasted young lady now sitting up on one side and a still passed out brunette on the other side. Grant put his index finger to his lips and said, "Keep quiet and you'll live through this."

The blond shrank back as Grant put his gun back in his pants, reached down and jerked the bedcovers off. He grabbed Batista by his ankles and dragged him to the foot of the bed before yanking him up and throwing him over his shoulder. As he exited the room he noticed the brunette young lady had not stirred.

Just after sun up the following morning a young man was helping his girlfriend walk over the lava bed rock outcropping that separated a public beach from a private beach. As they descended the rocks and landed on the beach they were greeted by a sign that read; 'Private Beach. No Trespassing!'

"Oh we should go back. We shouldn't be here," the young lady exclaimed.

"Don't be foolish. These rich bastards think they own the world," the boy replied grabbing her by the hand and pulling her.

"No!" she protested with a look of horror and pointing behind the boy at the base of the cliff.

The young man turned around and gasped. Tied to driftwood and propped up against the cliff stood three dead men. Their pants had been pulled down to their ankles, their penis' had been severed and inserted in their mouths and a sign around the one in the center read;

Beware; this is what will happen to anyone who deals in the sex trafficking of our young girls and daughters. We know who you are and we will find you and your fate will be the same as these pigs.

Victor Benitez paced nervously back and forth in his office at his residence in Acapulco, Mexico, on hold while the operator at the McCormick Place Hotel in Chicago, attempted to connect him to the room of Arturo Vasquez.

When a woman finally answered he said, "Rosa, its Victor and I need to talk to Senor Vasquez."

"I'm sorry Victor, but Senor Vasquez is in a meeting with a Turkish arms dealer and told me he didn't want to be disturbed," she replied.

Benitez winced and said, "Ooh Rosa, this is not a secured line. Be careful what you say," he admonished and then exclaimed, "Tell Senor Vasquez it is very important that I speak to him. I promise, you will not get in trouble."

"Okay, I'll see if he wants to talk to you."

He continued to pace and stopped when he heard a familiar voice, "Victor, this better be important."

"Oh it is," Benitez said and continued, "Jorge Batista and two of his men were found dead this morning. Can you call me back on a secure line?"

"Yes," Vasquez said and hung up.

A minute later Benitez's phone rang and he answered.

"Tell me about it," Vasquez ordered.

Benitez recounted how the bodies were found and that the police had no suspects and finished by saying, "Senor Vasquez, all of these slayings of our suppliers has to be more than a coincidence and now they have come close to home. I have doubled my personal security and I recommend you do the same. I also must tell you that our supply of product has come to a virtual standstill. Everyone is panicked by these death squads."

After a long pause Benitez inquired, "Senor Vasquez, are you still there?"

"Yes, yes," Vasquez answered perturbed, "I was thinking. All of this bull shit started after we started doing business with our new friend. Not only do I want you to cease doing business with him, but I want you and your men to visit this Mr. Smith at that house in Douglas and this time you will not fail to convince him to reveal our friend's identity. Do you understand me?"

"Si," Benitez replied as the phone connection went dead.

In the suite next to the one occupied by Vasquez and his people, Ian took off the earphone connected to a black box with a small antenna attached. Turning toward Jesse he said, "It's time to pull up stakes in Douglas. Please call Brown and have the team meet us here. Tell him to leave Grant behind to clean up our business. Mr. Smith, I think it's about time Senior Vasquez meets his new friend."

Just after eleven o'clock that night, crouched down in the far end of the beet field, Grant squatted watching through night vision glasses three dark colored SUVs speeding down the driveway to the ranch style home and then as they stopped in front of the garage. Men exited from all of the vehicles armed with fully automatic weapons and they surrounded the house. Victor Benitez opened the door of the last SUV and stepped out holding a bull horn. He was about to speak into it when Grant removed his night vision glasses, depressed a button on the remote control he was carrying and said, "Adios."

Benitez first sensed total silence and the blissfulness of flying unabated through the air as if he had defied the laws of gravity. The next thing he felt was an intense heat and pain. His sense of hearing returned and he heard loud screams, and panic set in as he wondered if he was in hell. His last living sensation was the realization that the screams he was hearing were his own.

Grant watched as the night sky before him lit up as the fifty gallon barrel of napalm in the garage ignited an instant after the explosion. He cupped his ears with his hands, turned away and tightly closed his eyes in anticipation of the ensuing loud boom, the concussion and rush of hot air.

He calmly stood and walked up the embankment behind him and lifted his off road motor cycle from the tall grass next to the irrigation canal and donning a helmet he kick started the bike. He turned for a last look at the devastation he was leaving behind. Where the house and garage once sat was now just level ground with a few small burning piles of timber. The three SUVs were only crumpled and smoldering frames lying at odd angles on the scorched earth. That was the great thing about napalm, Grant was thinking, it burns with such intense heat it consumes the surrounding oxygen it requires to burn and kills itself.

As he sped off down the canal access road he chuckled and whispered to himself, "That's kind of like you, Victor Benitez."

Arturo Vasquez was standing and looking over the shoulder of his vice-president of sales as the man explained a power point presentation of their newly introduced four point seat restraining belt designed for high end luxury sport automobiles to a team of design engineers from a Japanese car manufacturer. They were standing inside his booth in the south wing of the McCormick Place Convention Center at the International Trade Association's Annual Assembly.

Out of the corner of his eye something caught his attention and following a double take he recognized the man he knew only as Mr. Smith. He politely excused himself from the group and walked over to him and extending his hand, said, "Mr. Smith, so nice to see you again."

Jesse shook his hand and said, "I assume you have not heard yet,"

"Heard what?"

"Is there a place we can speak in private," Jess inquired.

Vasquez led him to the rear corner of the booth and ushered him into a glassed in corner office. Still standing behind his desk he asked, "Now, what is it you have to say?"

"Maybe you should sit down," Jesse replied.

"I'll remain standing, thank you."

"Well," Jesse began, "You were warned that your new friend preferred to remain anonymous and yet you have persisted in trying to find out who he is. I'm afraid your curiosity had led to the untimely death of your friend Victor Benitez and twelve or thirteen of his soldiers. The exact number has not been established yet. The authorities are still sifting through the rubble trying to identify charred body parts."

The smile on Vasquez's face had turned to a scowl and as he dialed a number on his cell phone he growled, "That's nonsense."

He turned his back to Jesse and the only thing Jesse could hear him say was, "Why was I not notified immediately?"

He turned around slowly and slumping down into his chair he looked up at Jesse with a mixture of fear and curiosity in his eyes and asked, "What is it you want?"

"It is fairly simple," Jesse continued unaffected, "it seems with the loss of El Diablo's Jorge Batista and now your man Victor, your distribution of product is in a world of hurt. Couple that with the fact that your pipeline to parts south has been cut off, I'd say you're in big trouble."

"I'm assuming you have a solution," Vasquez said respectfully.

"That's where the good news comes in, Senor Vasquez. You see, to this point your morbid curiosity as to who your new friend is has resulted in the unnecessary deaths of some good men, but that's about to change. He'd like to meet you under one condition."

"And what would that condition be?"

"Only that you agree to discuss the possibility of a partnership agreement in good faith. You see, your friend likes to know his partners. If you agree, I'm to invite you to a private dinner tonight in his suite at the McCormick," Jesse said as he slid a small envelope across the desk.

"You mean he wants me to work for him."

"A partnership," Jesse simply replied.

"Please tell him I would be very happy to discuss in good faith a mutual partnership relationship with him and I will be there tonight."

—

Vasquez and his large companion stood in front of the suite door and knocked. The door was opened by Jesse and he said, "Senior Vasquez, please come in. I don't believe I've met your companion."

The two men entered the room and Vasquez said, "This is my personal assistant, Hector Chavez."

Standing in the corner of the room with his back to the group and looking out of the window at the Chicago skyline, Ian O'Farrell turned and smiling said, "Ah, Senor Vasquez, we finally meet. Can I get you something to drink?"

"I'm not here for a social visit," Vasquez scowled and continued, "Let's cut through the bull shit. You have effectively shut down my ability to conduct one facet of my business. I suspect you plan on taking over my operation, so I don't see any reason why you would need me in any kind of partnership. So that leaves me to question, who are you and why am I here?"

Ian walked over, stood in front of him and nodding said, "Those are fair questions, my friend and I will cut through the bull shit and will do my best to answer them. First; you may find this unbelievable, but I work for a group who is dedicated to putting an end to the sick business you conduct."

Vasquez looked at him confused and before he could respond, Ian pulled out a hand gun from beneath his jacket and held the barrel against Vasquez's forehead. Hector reacted by reaching under his shirt and suddenly froze feeling the barrel of Jesse's pistol pressed against his temple. Jesse reached down with his free hand and removed Hector's sidearm from his waistband.

"The answer to your second question," Ian said smiling, "is, I lied. You are here to be arrested and eventually to be tried, convicted and one day be executed for your crimes."

Mary Dinosa and Joan Richards stepped out from the adjoining room and swiftly walked across the room, both holding a pair of handcuffs. Richards approached Vasquez and grabbing a wrist and yanking it behind his back, said, "Arturo Vasquez, you are under arrest."

Dinosa did the same to Hector as Vasquez protested, "I don't know who you are, but I'm in this country with a diplomatic immunity passport. You are not authorized to arrest me!"

With Vasquez now handcuffed, Richards produced two folded pieces of paper from her vest pocket and slamming one down on the table in front of them she growled, "This is an order from our State Department revoking your diplomatic status," and slamming the other paper down she added, "And this is an arrest warrant issued by our Justice Department."

Turning toward Ian, Dinosa said, "You two should get the hell out of here. FBI Agents are on their way."

After Ian kissed her, he and Jesse walked to the front door and before leaving, Jesse turned and addressed the befuddled Vasquez, "Adios Senor Vasquez, and I hope you enjoy your stay in America."

―

"Mr. Schwartz, have you heard?" Rusk said into his phone.

"Yes, I've heard," Schwartz groaned.

"Then I think it's time you had that little chat with your boss and I would suggest you do not blow this," Rusk said with a hint of glee in his voice.

Schwartz hung up the phone, unloosened his tie and unbuttoned his top button. He pinned the American flag symbol provided by the FBI to his lapel and walked across the room to the adjoining door connecting his office to Senator Abrams' office.

A pretty young assistant sat with a steno pad on her lap next to the Senator's desk taking dictation from her boss when Schwartz said, "Excuse me Barbara, but I have something important to discuss with the Senator. Could you give us a moment?"

She politely excused herself and after she had left the room, Abrams said, "Jesus Ralph, I was dictating my acceptance speech for the Rotary Club's humanitarian of the year award tonight."

Ignoring his comment, Schwartz sat down on the vacated chair and said, "I'm afraid we have bigger problems than that. Arturo Vasquez had just been arrested by the FBI."

A look of shock and surprise crossed Abrams' face and he responded, "That's impossible! I would have been informed."

"Well, it's happened and you know what that can mean," Schwartz said shaking his head.

"What about his diplomatic Visa? I lobbied hard to get that for him. I demand answers!"

"That by itself presents a problem. There will be a paper trail back to you for that effort, but what if he starts talking about your other involvements?"

Abrams looked around bewildered. He slapped his forehead and finally uttered, "Holy shit! He could reveal his illegal contributions to my campaigns. How do I explain the yacht, my home in Beverly Hills, the Bahama vacation house, the cars, the lavish vacations and all the rest? Tell me they can't trace that. Tell me we can always claim credible deniability."

A half a dozen FBI agents dressed in full SWAT gear followed by a sleepy eyed, dedicated Joan Richards burst through the outer office of the Senator's suite and, amidst screams from secretaries and assistants, proceeded to Abrams' office. Entering, Richards, flashing her FBI badge, cried, "Senator John Quincy Abrams, you're under arrest for treason against the United States of America and about a zillion other counts!"

Now standing and being cuffed, Abrams looked across his desk at Ralph Schwartz and with a look of sudden realization he roared, "You son of a bitch!"

Richards handed another piece of paper to Schwartz saying, "This is a warrant authorizing us to search the Senator's office. Similar warrants are now being served at his office in Washington, his home, his condo in D.C., his yacht, his place in Bermuda and all of his vehicles are being impounded, including his wife's brand new chauffeur-driven Rolls Royce."

Abrams head sagged with his chin resting on his chest as he was escorted shamelessly by four members of SWAT through his maze of offices and open mouthed staff members, into the outside hallway where he was greeted by dozens of yelling reporters and camera crews.

Ian, Jesse, Grant and Brown sat around a table playing cards while Dinosa was fast asleep snuggled under a blanket in her reclined seat inside the cabin of the corporate jet.

Ian played a card and said, "Hey Grant, I read the report on your cleanup job in Texas. I'm not surprised it was excellent work."

"Yeah, when do I get issued my cape?" Grant grunted a reply.

"You know, you might look good in a Superman cape, but the thought of you running around in tights scares me to death," Jesse remarked.

As loud laughter erupted from the group, Dinosa rolled over in her seat and hollered, "Keep it down, dammit!"

As the laughter died down it was interrupted when Ian's phone rang. It was George Armstrong.

"Where are you guys?" he asked.

Peering out of a cabin window and looking down, Ian replied, "From the looks of it, we're somewhere over Colorado approaching the Rocky Mountain. We're heading to Las Vegas for a day or two of R and R."

"Sorry to disrupt your plans, but another situation has come up and we need you back here. It seems some self-claimed prophet from Allah and chief of a Muslim terrorist army in Nigeria has kidnapped several hundred school girls. How soon can you be at my house?"

"We can land at SFO in about two hours and we'll come directly to your place," Ian replied.

—

CHAPTER FIFTEEN

The corporate jet taxied onto the tarmac and pulled up in front of the large 'Armstrong Enterprises, Inc.' hangar. An SUV and a limousine were parked next to it and the two drivers were engaged in a conversation outside and between the two vehicles. As the passengers deplaned, Valerie Kane emerged from the rear of the limo and approached Dinosa.

"It's good to have you back home," she said as the two women hugged.

Stepping back, Dinosa sighed, "It's good to be home. It has been a long couple of weeks and I'm exhausted, but I know you don't want to hear about it."

"Not a word," Kane said sternly, "But I have a lot to catch you up on."

After her luggage was unloaded from the jet and reloaded in the trunk of the limo, Dinosa crawled into the back seat, laid her head back, closed her eyes and said, "Let's hear it."

"Well, as you can imagine, the office has been a zoo. I've assigned two full time ADAs and a pool of assistants to work with the feds coordinating and preparing their prosecutions. They all report every day to the Federal Building.

"We've been assigned the prosecutions of mostly low level local crime figures; the gang thugs, some of the pimps and their customers, escort service operators and cab drivers who received kickbacks for delivering customers. The problem is, and I suppose you can call it a good problem, is these creeps are rolling over faster than pins at a professional bowling tournament.

"Between us and the feds we've developed several suspect pyramids that would rival the White House lawn Christmas tree and more complicated than an L.A. freeway interchange. So far we've identified and plan to prosecute over one thousand people nationwide and the list grows by the hour.

"I take it you've heard about Senator Abrams and his Chief of Staff?"

After Dinosa nodded and indicated she had, Kane continued, "Yesterday we busted a California State Senator from our district that's not only implicated in the sex slave industry, but and also connected with gun running activities by the Huang Tong."

"I know I'm needed, but is there a chance I could just go home and get some rest and report for work in the morning?" Dinosa sighed.

"Does the Pope shit in the forest?" Kane retorted.

—

The weary warriors were met by George Armstrong in the foyer of his manor, "Welcome home boys. Just leave your gear here and follow me. Everybody's in the den."

As they trudged through the hall to the den, Jesse turned to Brown and pointing at Grant who was just ahead of them, chuckled, "Can you imagine that fat ass in leotards?"

"I heard that Leone," Grant complained.

When they entered the den they were greeted by Bernard Rusk, Solomon Goldsmith and Ian O'Farrell. After hugs and congratulations were shared, Rusk flipped on the large screen television with the remote. It showed the inside ruins of what had once been a school room. Desks were overturned and debris littered the floor of the scorched room. Rusk toggled through more scenes of what appeared to be a ransacked school.

"This is what is left of a girl's school located just north of Lagos, Nigeria. It was raided by a group of Islamic terrorists a week ago yesterday. The school was trashed, sixteen teachers and school staff members were slaughtered and over three hundred school girls, ranging in ages twelve through sixteen, were kidnapped," Rusk began.

"The group known as Boca Haram is led by an Al Qaeda backed self-proclaimed army general named Boza Faq Nakimbo. He and his followers are believers in radical Sharia Islamic law. They believe all who do not believe and follow Sharia must be converted or eliminated. They teach that women are totally subservient to man and for a girl or woman to educate or to be educated is a mortal sin and that they have been selected to carry out Allah's sentence.

"Of course, these hypocritical bastards have no problem with raping and torturing these girls and selling them to become whores and concubines. This atrocity has just been released to the public and has stirred international furor and outrage," Rusk paused, turned his head, gritted his teeth and with controlled anger continued;

"Our present Administration in disinclined to get involved. Our current foreign policy is to not interfere with other country's internal problems. We are no longer the international police, or so goes the rhetoric. Eventually this story will fade from the headlines and the chances that these girls will be rescued are slim. That, gentlemen, is where we come into the picture."

"Just how many men are in this Bozo Fuck's army?" Grant asked, soliciting several chuckles from the group.

"Our intelligence says he's recruited about eight hundred followers. Some are dedicated religious fanatics, but most of them are like their leader. Local thugs who enjoy massacring innocent men and women and partying with their daughters by raping and torturing them in mass orgies," Rusk replied bitterly.

He continued, "This group is funded and has been armed by the central arm of Al Qaeda in Iran and Syria, but most of their funds come from strong arm robberies of banks, retail establishments and extortion and sex slave trafficking. This asshole Nakimbo is nothing more than a punk committing diabolical crimes under the guise of being a prophet of Allah."

Rusk flipped on the large screen monitor that displayed a satellite view of a town identified as Baga, Nigeria, next to Chad Lake in the country's northeast corner. Indicating with the cursor, Rusk started, "This is the town of Baga. It's located in the northeastern corner of Nigeria at its border with Chad. Baga is a poor fishing village with a population of over seventeen thousand residents. A little over a year ago a Nigerian military patrol was attacked by Nakimbo's men just outside of town and although there are conflicting reports, the army chased the terrorists back into town and killed several civilians and torched as many as thirty homes.

"That action resulted in the conversion of many of the town's citizens to Boca Haram sympathizers. They were rewarded by Nakimbo taking hostage over three hundred of their daughters from a Christian school last week. The area has become a hot bed for Boca Haram terrorists and this," he explained moving the cursor to a peninsula bordering the lake less than five mile southeast of the town, "is one of his compound headquarters."

Zooming in on the peninsula, he continued, "As you can see, the compound is surrounded on three sides by the lake and is well fortified. A ten foot high electrified fence crosses the land entrance and here you can see fortified bunkers armed with thirty caliber machine guns, mortars and militants with automatic rifles and grenade launchers."

Rusk zoomed into the center of the compound and pointing the cursor at a group of thatched covered buildings he started, "These buildings are barracks, and this large one here near the center is where we believe the surviving girls are being held."

He moved the cursor to a large villa near the water's edge and said, "This is the residence of Nakimbo."

Brown interrupted and commented, "You said the surviving girls. Does that mean some of the girls are already dead?"

Rusk zoomed the image back out and moved the scene to about one mile south of the compound and zoomed in on what appeared to be a filled in trench that stretched a length of approximately two hundred feet.

"We don't know the number exactly, but from eye witness accounts, we believe over half of the girls were slaughtered two days after they were taken and buried here. Probably because they were deemed trouble makers, refused to convert or wouldn't fetch much from the black market," Rusk remarked.

"I call first dibs at this mother fucker," Jesse spat out.

"The surviving girls we think have at least outwardly converted to Muslim. Some may have succumbed to the Stockholm syndrome and actually believe and some may be in a survival mode and just pretending. We have developed a plan to rescue them. It will be a very difficult and dangerous operation and the chances that all of you will be returning home are slim. If you volunteer for this mission, make sure your personal business and Wills are in order.

"Above all, the girl's safety is the main priority and if at any time things should go south you are to abort the mission. If that happens, it's a good chance our ability to extract you will be slim and you'll be on your own. Does everybody understand?" Rusk asked, looking at each man as they nodded acknowledgement.

"Okay, that said, you'll be happy to learn that you will not be alone on the ground. Believe it or not, there is another group, much like yourselves, comprised of four young men from various parts of the British Commonwealth. They include two Brits, one Canadian and one Aussie. They'll be arriving later this afternoon and we'll go over the mission together.

"Now, I suggest you all get some rest, and if any of you decide to opt out of this, let me know and it will be completely understood."

Several hours later the team was summoned to the home's basement gymnasium and was introduced to their four new members. They were;

Mike Carpenter, a thirty-two year old from South Wales stood a solid six feet two inches and gave the impression he was a proper English gentleman. The team would learn he was anything but that. He had served eight years in the Royal Army Special Forces and had participated or led secret counter intelligence operations all over the world.

James Finnegan was Carpenter's opposite from a London suburb. He stood about five feet eight inches, was a former high school wrestling champ and with his cockney accent appeared to be a street wise hooligan. At twenty-eight years old, a crooked nose and scars over both eyes, he looked like somebody who'd been around the block and not to be messed with. He also served four years under the command of Carpenter.

Garrett Moore was from British Columbia, Canada. He was thirty years old and was raised on the coast in a small logging community. He grew up in a family of four brothers and two sisters and learned early on how to survive in the wild, developing hunting and fishing skills. He was a pleasant looking man, but powerfully built on a sturdy six foot frame. He joined the Canadian Army at the age of eighteen and because of his special skills was recruited by Carpenter during a joint operation in Afghanistan and attached to his team.

Erick Von Strudt was the man from Australia. Tall and wiry, he moved with the agility of a panther stalking its prey. He was the youngest team member at twenty-seven and as an orphan he caught the eye of a British nobleman and agent for MI-6 who took the then nineteen year old youth under his wing and brought him back to England to be trained by the military in special tactics and eventually made up a part of his independent team. The British member of MI-6 and nobleman's name was Lord Jonathan Washburn.

Following introductions, they all sat down in fold up chairs facing a large screen television and paid attention to Rusk who was standing next to the monitor. Three hours later he concluded the session saying, "Alright, we'll break for dinner and then meet back here for final instructions and questions. I understand George is grilling up some great steaks on the deck."

As the group broke up and moved upstairs and out toward the back deck, Ian stepped aside and returned a voice mail message left by Dinosa.

"Hey Babe, what's up?" he said.

"Oh hi Honey," she replied with a sigh, "I'm at home in my office going over the reports and indictments Val gave me and trying to make sense of them.

Her demeanor changed to excitement when she continued and exclaimed, "You won't believe what the Feds are going to prosecute Senator Abrams for. Among a long list of other crimes, they allege he committed treason against the United States and conspiracy of illegal slave trafficking and conspiracy to commit murder. The Attorney General is seeking the death penalty. Homeland Security wants to add aiding and abetting a terrorist organization charges. His Chief of Staff, Ralph Schwartz, has pled guilty to similar charges and in exchange for his cooperation has agreed to serve a fifty to life sentence. He'll be an old limber dick before he's even considered for parole.

"Arturo Vasquez is facing the death penalty for you name it, he did it. He's trying to pull all the political strings in his country and has petitioned the United Nations for political asylum status. Fortunately, especially since those girls in Nigeria were kidnapped and being threatened with being sold into slavery, he's pissing into the wind and he might as well bend over, stick his head between his legs and kiss his ass good-bye."

She paused, waiting for a response and when none came, she whined, "Ian, when are you coming home. I need a little hubba-hubba."

Ian chuckled, bringing back memories of Mary's old homicide partner in the SFPD, Chuck Chalmers. During their wedding reception, to the embarrassment of old Chuck and his wife, their daughter had one too many glasses of champagne and chiding her parents revealed, when she was younger, her parents referred to that term thinking their daughter wouldn't know their intentions.

"I'm not sure, but don't wait up for me," Ian replied.

"This wouldn't have anything to do with those girls in Africa, would it?" she asked coyly and then added, "I heard Rusk is in town."

"Probably best you not ask, dear."

"Yeah, yeah, I know, but you're gonna miss some great hubba-hubba," she giggled.

"Well, don't start without me. I love you," Ian said hanging up.

He joined the group on the back patio and was approached by Mike Carpenter who shook his hand and said jovially, "Well, I finally get to meet the infamous Yank, Colonel Ian O'Farrell."

"Actually, we came close to meeting one time in Syria. My team," he indicated Grant and Jesse, "provided cover and sniper fire when you and your men rescued those Red Cross workers in that village. That would have been about six years ago," Ian commented.

"I often wondered if that was you, but with all the hush-hush surrounding that mission I never could ascertain exactly who covered our rear. Allow me now the opportunity to thank you. You and your men saved our butts that day," Carpenter remarked and turning toward his men he bellowed, "Hey guys, these are the men that covered and saved our arses several years ago in Al Tabqah, Syria, when we extracted those Red Cross blokes!"

Back slaps, hugs and handshakes between the men followed Carpenter's announcement and an air of jubilance filled the atmosphere as the men swapped old war stories and enjoyed their meal and new found camaraderie. As the group co-mingled and shared conversation, it turned out virtually all of the men had resigned their military positions as a frustrating result of political interference and rules of engagement and had found a more rewarding opportunity to serve their countries and humanity.

—

CHAPTER SIXTEEN

The C130 cargo jet cut through the night sky at an elevation of fifteen thousand feet. The planes transponder transmitted a signal that indicated the plane was at thirty thousand feet along with a signal identifying it as a commercial airliner on a scheduled flight from Johannesburg, South Africa to Tel Aviv, Israel. Aboard in the cargo area were the eight crusaders dressed in dark jungle camouflaged fatigues with similarly decorated charcoal painted faces and hands. They remained silent, internalizing their thoughts to the task ahead.

Each man wore an armored vest, a parachute jump helmet along with a parachute pack strapped to their backs and an AR-16 rifle attached to their chests with an easy brake away snap. On their waist belts they all carried a Colt .45 with attached silencers and five fifteen round clips. In their laps sat fifty pound packs filled with munitions and supplies that were tethered to their ankles to be released after their chutes deployed. Strapped on each of their wrists was a three inch by three inch GPS monitor that indicated their present location, altitude, and bright spots showed the position of their seven other comrades. One of the spots was red that indicated the position of Alpha team leader, Ian O'Farrell. Another was green indicating Bravo team leader, Mike Carpenter. Each device also doubled as a radio and along with ear plug phones, would allow voice communication between the team members within a range of two miles.

Suddenly the rear cargo door began to open and a rush of cool air purged the cabin. Carpenter yelled, "Beta team, get ready," and he stood and moved toward the rear. His three friends followed in single file and they looked like a line of slow moving bow legged turtles as they waddled toward the open cargo door. Carpenter was the first to dive out of the plane in a belly flop posture. One by one the others followed and they disappeared into the darkness.

Approximately three minutes later Ian bellowed out, "Alpha team, get ready!" and the four men performed the same ritual. Following the deployment of their chutes the three followers kept an eye on their GPSs and directed their descent to trail their leader at predetermined intervals.

The plan called for Beta team, once safely on the ground, to proceed to the front of the rebel compound, conceal themselves and await further orders. Alpha team would land at the edge of Lake Chad several miles east and inflate the pair of self-inflatable two man rafts. They would paddle their crafts around to the compound's peninsula point and conduct a covert beach attack.

When they had maneuvered their rafts approximately one hundred yards from the beach, Ian signaled Grant and Jesse to swing east in their raft and he and Brown proceeded toward the beach. It was three o'clock in the morning and except for a few lights illuminating the center of the compound, the shoreline was dark.

Over their ear phones they heard a cackle and then, "Beta team in position."

A low marsh fog lay over the lake and the dark silhouette of the peninsula appeared through their night vision glasses as Ian and Brown slowly and quietly paddled their raft toward the muddy and rocky beach on the west bank. From viewing multiple satellite images of the compound, they knew it was protected from a lake side attack by three guarded outposts. One was located at the tip of the peninsula at the foot of a pier and the other two protected each flank. The posts were manned by two guards behind stacks of sand bags and they were armed with thirty caliber machine guns and mortar launchers.

The assault plan called for Ian and Brown to take out the guard post to the west and Jesse and Grant to do the same on the east bank. The posts were each located within fifty yards from the pier guards and to avoid detection from that position, they knew the job would require silent stealth. After dispatching the threat of the two positions, they would meet at the pier and eliminate the guards there.

Ian and Brown landed behind a rocky out cropping and pulled their raft ashore. They crawled into the jungle and crept silently toward the guard post. Both men now unsheathed their combat knives when they emerged from the bush and saw the two guards only thirty feet away with their backs propped up against the sand bags and snoring contentedly.

Ian looked at Brown with a cynical smile and shook his head. They ditched their backpacks and inched forward in a belly crawl until they were only several feet from the slumbering guards. Looking again at Brown and receiving a nod, Ian mouthed, "Now," and the two men sprung forward. Ian grabbed his man around the head and covered his mouth with his hand to muffle a grunt, wrapped his legs around the man's mid-section and jerked his head back while simultaneously drawing his knife across the man's throat severing his jugular and windpipe. He held the man in place until the body spasms stopped. Brown did the same to his man.

They retrieved their backpacks and crept toward the pier when they heard a series of plinks and paused. Continuing on, they met Grant and Jesse at the path to the pier. Grant whispered, "All guards are eliminated."

The end of the path found the compound's center, framed on both sides with two long narrow barracks, a larger one in the center and a munitions depot in the far corner. To the east was a villa that sat on the edge of the peninsula's bay. The men quickly dispersed, each going to an assigned soldier's barracks and planted bricks of C-2 from the open crawl spaces beneath and at each end of the structures. After attaching remote detonators, the group reformed in front of larger barracks where the kidnapped girls were being held.

Ian nodded at Brown who immediately dashed quietly across the compound toward the villa. The windows on the barracks were open and barred from the outside. Crouched down outside the entrance door, Ian hand gestured Grant to go to the nearest window and look in. After peering through the window, Grant turned and held up his index finger, indicating one guard, and then with his palms together and his hands pressed against his cheek, he signaled the man was asleep. Ian gestured with his hand in the shape of a pistol and after Grant nodded, he withdrew his sidearm, aimed it through the window and pulled the trigger, sending the hapless guard into a sleep he would never awake. He whispered to himself, "I hope your seventy-seven virgins are fat, ugly and nag you to death."

Ian spoke into his wrist radio, "Beta team, commence."

Carpenter came back, "Roger."

The three men entered the barracks. There were four rows of cots and they moved to the nearest one. Grant cupped the mouth of the sleeping girl and when her terrified eyes opened, he said in a low calming voice, "Please do not worry. We are friends here to rescue you and the others. Do you speak English?"

Her eyes relaxed and Grant removed his hand. She couldn't have been more than sixteen years old, but she sat up in bed and defiantly said, "I speak perfect English. Where have you been?"

Grant smiled and replied, "We're here now, honey. Do you think you could quietly awaken the other girls and tell them to pass the word and get dressed? How many are you and are all the girls here?"

"Two girls are at the General's villa, but the others who have survived are here and I will waken them. There are ninety-eight of us. Are you going to return us to our parents?" she replied.

He nodded yes and turned toward Ian who said, "You guys get the girls ready to move," and he dashed outside.

He met Brown coming across the compound and told him they would have to return to the villa and rescue two other girls. When they reached the stairs leading up to the porch and entrance, Ian signaled Brown to circle around to the rear of the house. He crept up the stairs and seeing no guards he walked silently to the front door and whispered into his radio for Brown to enter the rear door.

With his pistol drawn and held at his cheek, he entered the home and at the other end of a hall he saw Brown enter from the rear. Ian found himself standing in a room that housed a kitchen and front room and the hall at the other side that extended to where Brown now stood. They both started moving toward one another and Ian cringed at the floor creaking noises that came with each step.

Suddenly a door off the hall opened and a naked Boza Faq Nakimbo stepped out with pistol in hand and demanded, "Who's there?"

Two plinks rang out and the great General fell to the floor with one bullet hole to the front and one to the back of his head. His body jerked uncontrollably for a moment before it went still and his eye balls rolled up into their sockets.

Brown hurried to the bedroom door and looked in at two frozen and terrified young girl sitting up in bed. He holstered his pistol and slowly approaching the girls he whispered, "Its' okay girls, we're here to take you and your friends back to your families."

He picked up the two burkas lying on a chair in the corner, handed them to the girls and turning his back to them, said, "Please, put these on and come with us."

He noticed Ian in the hallway picking up Nakimbo's body and throwing him over his shoulder and asked, "What the hell are you doing?"

"I thought we'd leave a little message for his friends," Ian replied.

He waited for Brown to escort the two girls out of the house and then followed them back to the others who were gathered inside the girl's barracks. As they waited to hear from Beta team, Ian asked where he might find a pencil and paper. One of the girls pointed at the dead guard and Ian retrieved a pen from the man's breast pocket and a notebook from the thigh pocket of his fatigue trousers and scribbled on a piece of paper;

Beware; this is what will happen to anyone who deals in the sex trafficking of our young girls and daughters. We know who you are and we will find you and your fate will be the same as this pig.

He folded the paper and placed it in his pocket when he heard in his ear phone, "Alpha team, this is Beta team. The front gate is secured."

He opened the door and Jesse and Grant led the girls out and they dashed quickly and quietly toward the front of the compound. Ian picked up the body of Nakimbo and he and Brown followed the group protecting their rear. They met up with Carpenter and his team who were all on one knee with their rifles trained toward the soldier's barracks. A hint of daylight was beginning to appear over the hills on the far side of the lake. Two dead soldiers lay twisted in each of the gate side bunkers.

Ian slung Nakimbo up against the barbed wire gate and the naked body became impaled there. He removed the note paper from his pocket and with a pen knife he attached it to the dead man's chest. A few of the young girls walked up and spit on the gross and now harmless corpse.

Peering over his shoulder, Carpenter remarked, "Nice touch, Governor."

Lights began to appear through the windows of the barracks and Ian said, "You better get the girls out of here."

He and Brown remained behind and when the others had disappeared off the dirt road and down a path, the two men relocated behind a large oak tree and produced remote detonators from their packs and flipped a switch. A red light appeared on each device and after nodding at each other they depressed a button.

The dark sky lit up like the finale of the fireworks display over the Chesapeake Bay on the Fourth of July. Secondary explosions from the munitions depot dwarfed the already bright horizon. When Brown and Ian looked around from the protection of the tree and after the smoke cleared, only devastation lay before them. All of the buildings were completely leveled and even the two and a half ton halftrack vehicles were unrecognizable with parts strewn across the seared grounds.

"Damn," Brown exclaimed, "What the hell did they have in that ammunition dump?"

"God only knows," Ian remarked and added, "But I'll make sure to thank Him in my prayers tonight."

They waited to see if any survivors might present a threat and when they saw and heard nothing, Ian raised his wrist to his mouth and said, "Beta team, what's your location?"

Carpenter replied, "We're less than a quarter mile from the extraction point. We did pause to watch the fireworks extravaganza you chaps put on. Again, good show."

"When you reach the clearing, go ahead and signal for the choppers and prepare the girls. We're on our way and should be joining you in about ten minutes," Ian said.

Ian and Brown took a final look at what was once a Boca Haram military compound, then turned and started jogging and followed the path their comrades and the girls had taken. About a mile from them, the team and girls crouched at the edge of the clearing where just a week before over two hundred of the girl's friends and classmates were buried in a long trench.

Von Strudt sprinted to the middle of the field and shot an orange colored flare into the sky and scattered several other orange smoke flares on the ground while the rest of the team separated and organized the girls in groups of twenty.

"This is Los Santos," everyone heard over their ear phones. "We're observing live satellite feed of your position and approximately a dozen troop trucks containing about two hundred Boca Haram soldiers have just arrived at the compound and are headed in your direction. Their ETA is about ten to fifteen minutes. We're trying to arrange support, but you cannot rely on it."

Ian took a moment to think and then radioed, "Beta team, leave one man to help load the girls and the rest of you come our way. We'll meet you on the path."

He and Brown then looked about them and seeing a slight rise just ahead, Brown said, "It ain't the greatest spot to repel two hundred enemy soldiers, but beggars can't be choosers and I don't think from this vantage they'll have a visual of the copters."

Ian nodded and they began planting several anti-personnel mines along the trail and in the surrounding bush. After ordering a reluctant Von Strudt to stay behind and assist the girls, Carpenter and the others ran back down the trail toward their friends.

When they reached Ian and Brown they spread out and began laying anti-personnel mines scattering them on the path and into the bush and then regrouped around Ian. The sound of multiple helicopters could be heard approaching to their rear.

"Okay, we need to occupy these guys for about ten minutes. On my command, everybody will fall back to the extraction point. Myself," he paused and after receiving a knowing look from Grant, he continued, "and Grant will provide cover. Now let's spread out on that rise over there."

They waited and watched as the first group of enemy soldiers came jogging down the path in single file. The lead man stepped on a mine and the explosion hurled his legless body into the air. The seven team members opened fire with short bursts from their automatic rifles, killing and wounding several other bewildered men. More mines were detonated as the soldiers dispersed into the bush. There was only sporadic return fire from the enemy and Ian ordered, "Fall back!"

Ian and Grant remained at their positions as the rest of their team picked up their gear and sprinted to the path and back toward the clearing. The sound of departing helicopters could be heard in the background when everyone heard in their earphones, "The girls are clear. Proceed to the clearing and wait for pick-up."

Several more mines detonated in the bush and Ian knew the main body of the enemy troops was on scene, spread out and closing in on them. He looked at Grant who was located on the opposite side of the path and spoke into his radio, "Grant, fall back and cover."

It was a typical command and maneuver by which a two man team would retreat from an enemy advancement. One would cover the other and then overlap each other in a slow retreat. Grant grabbed his gear and sprinted to the rear as Ian opened fire spraying the area to his front.

The other team members reached the clearing and were greeted by Von Strudt. "What the hell are you doing here?" Carpenter demanded.

"As the Yanks would say, no soldier left behind, sir."

Carpenter shook his head and ordered the men to spread out along the clearing's edge when they heard, "This is Los Santos. Your pick-up chopper is inbound and we have two drones armed with napalm payload missiles positioned and waiting for you to direct their fire."

The panting voice of Ian came over the radio, "Carpenter, when the chopper arrives, load up and wait for us no more than one minute. If we don't show up, get the hell out of here, copy?"

After Carpenter affirmed, Ian continued over the crackling sounds of automatic fire, "Los Santos, have the chopper land in the center of the clearing. Drones, stand-by and wait for my command and direction of fire."

The Apache helicopter approached at tree top level from the east and sat down in the middle of the clearing. Carpenter and his men rushed toward it and everyone hopped on board except for Jesse and James Finnegan, who took kneeling positions outside of the opened doors.

"Drones, direct fire at the path fifty meters into the bush and spread hits for maximum efficiency and commence fire when ready,"

"Shit, he's calling for fire on his own position. They'll be cooked!" Jesse yelled.

"Look!" Carpenter marveled.

Appearing at the edge of the clearing they saw Grant limping along with Ian over his shoulder as smoke trails from the drone fired missiles zipped by over their heads. Grant threw Ian to the ground and covered him as the bush and jungle behind them erupted in a ball of fire.

Jesse and Finnegan began running to the fallen men whose position disappeared in a surge of smoke. The men continued running and as the smoke began to dissipate they were able to see a limping and coughing Grant struggling to drag his wounded buddy.

When they met, Jesse grabbed an unconscious Ian and rolled him up on his shoulder and yelled at Grant, "No, not the leg again?!"

He was referring that on two prior missions Grant had received leg wounds, but this time Grant was too exhausted to respond. Finnegan propped him up on his wounded side and they followed Jesse and Ian back to the safety of the helicopter and out of harm's way.

—

The four Apache helicopters carrying the confused, but hopeful girls, flew west at tree top level in a scattered formation. An hour later they hovered over the soccer field of the Sport Club's soccer field in Kano, Nigeria, and sat down in the middle of the circled landing zone surrounded by a ring of Nigerian Army regulars. Hundreds of anxious family members, onlookers and media reporters with camera crews crowded around the perimeter.

When the helicopter door opened and the girls began to file out, the crowd burst through the outer ring of soldiers and engulfed the girls. Hysterical mothers screamed their daughter's names and looked wildly about for a response. When they were eventually reunited there were cries and tears of uncontrollable joy. As the word spread that these were the only survivors and the girls who had survived were located by their families, mothers and fathers who did not find their daughters began to realize the inevitable.

Mothers fell wailing and sobbing to the ground. Some just wandered about in a stupor and as one veteran British new correspondent, trying to stifle his own emotions, described the scene;

In all of the years of my reporting, I have never witnessed a scene of such mixed emotions. We are seeing the uncontrollable joy of parents and families being reunited with their rescued daughters versus the indescribable grief of those when they realize their daughters will not be coming home. The dichotomy is simply diabolical.

Several hundred miles to the west of Kano, the chopper carrying the recue team sat down on the deck of the USS Enterprise anchored off the African Gulf coast. It was greeted by teams of corpsman and doctors and standing behind the medical personnel were Bernard Rusk and Lord Jonathan Washburn.

Before exiting the cabin, Carpenter made his way forward and patting the pilot's shoulder he noticed the man was in his mid-sixties. Taken slightly aback, he never the less yelled above the engine and rotor noise, "Hey skipper, that was some flying and took some balls of steel!"

"Son," the old pilot relied, "that was a walk in the park. I was a med-i-vac chopper jockey in Viet Nam."

"None the less, I'd like to thank you and buy you a cup of tea."

"I'd prefer it if you pretended you never met me."

As soon as the landing zone was safely clear, he pulled the helicopter up and swung away in the direction they had arrived.

Grant and Ian were carried by stretcher to the ship's sick bay and the rest of the team followed Rusk and Washburn to a debriefing cabin. They were served a hot meal and beverage of their choice.

When the meal had been consumed, Rusk raised his glass and toasted, "To a job well done."

After a chorus of, "Here, hears," he continued, "Only a few people know who you are and what you did and it must remain that way. Not even the President of the United States knows, nor will he ever."

"And, I might add, neither does the Prime Minister," Washburn commented.

"Your presence on this ship is explained as you are an independent contractor team responding to a hydraulics problem in the engine room," Rusk went on to explain.

At that very moment at a hastily gathered morning press conference in Washington D.C., the President's Press Secretary was saying;

"As grateful as the President and all of us are to see the successful rescue of the hostages held girls in northern Nigeria, other than providing that nation with advisor and intelligence personal, the United States did not participate in the rescue effort. This is in keeping with the President's policy of not to interfere with other nation's internal affairs."

Later that afternoon the press corps in Kano was air lifted to the destroyed Boca Haram compound and a firsthand look at where the girls had been held hostage. The British correspondent peered over the shoulder of his camera man and watched the footage they had just taken.

It was a close-up shot and showed only a note attached by a pen knife to something. A thin trail of blood tracked down across the paper from the bottom of the blade. The lettering and content of the note was plain to read.

As the image panned back revealing the dead body of a naked black man impaled on a barbed wire gate, the commentator reported, "That is the message left for the world to see by the rescuers of the kidnapped girls safely returned earlier today to their parents in Kano, Nigeria. The body to which it is pinned is believed to be that of the military head of the Boca Haram terrorist organization, Boza Faq Nakimbo."

"Excellent Scott," the reporter commented to his cameraman, "Let's get this filed as soon as possible. I'm sure the network will blur out his wanker, but the message will still ring out loud and clear."

—

"We were conducting an overlap buddy retreat and it was working pretty well. We were able to keep the enemy at bay. I guess those guys weren't quite ready to meet their virgins. I had just passed Ian and after taking a firing position I turned and saw Ian was about to be overwhelmed on his right flank. About a dozen guys were closing in on him and when his rifle clip empties he grabbed his forty-five and started dropping them like flies. I opened up and it seemed like we had eliminated the immediate threat. I yelled, Go!

"That's when he radioed in and directed the drones to fire. When he turned to retreat, a wounded Boca tossed a grenade in his direction. It exploded behind him as he was running toward me and he went down. I shot the grenade tossing prick and went back and retrieved our unconscious friend and while running back to the clearing I took a bullet in my leg. I kept going and the next thing I remember was feeling a hell like heat and then we were hit from behind by something that felt like two three hundred pound linebackers. Lying on the ground we were surrounded by blinding smoke and I got up and started dragging Ian. Hell, I didn't even know if I was dragging him in the right direction.

"I thought I was dreaming when I saw this little prick," he said smiling and looking at Jesse and then pointing at Finnegan he continued, "and the Limey here."

The team was gathered in the cabin of the corporate jet that was about to make its' final descent into Heathrow Airport. Grant had just finished his narration, sitting back in his seat with his casted right leg propped up on the seat in front of him. Ian was still unconscious, but expected to make a full recovery, and lying on his belly on a stretcher at the rear of the cabin being fed from an IV bag dangling from a pole. His head was wrapped in bandages and his bare back side and legs were speckled with taped gauze pads.

"Well, it's not the first time this little prick saved your fat ass," Jesse retorted.

Suddenly Ian woke in a drug induced stupor and began to sing, "Roll me over in the clover. Roll me over, lay me down and do it again."

Brown was the first to reach him and bent down looking into his glazed eyes, said, "Hey Ian, how ya doin'?"

Ian craned his head up and trying to focus his eyes he slurred, "Hey Gary, how's it going? Where the hell are we? Jesus, could you help me roll over?"

From behind them, Carpenter said, "Sorry old chap, but it'll be a while before that happens."

The End

EPILOGUE

Dinosa stood at the desk in the conference room at St. Leo's Sanctuary House and rolled out a thick set of architectural blue prints. Joan Richards, Sister Madelyn and several other Nuns gathered around her. The cover page was titled 'St. Leo's Sanctuary House New West Side Addition' and showed an aerial view, three dimensional drawing of a two story building covering the entire block across the street where currently sat empty warehouses. The center of the building was covered by a large opaque dome.

Pointing at it, Dinosa said excitingly, "Under that dome there will be a garden plaza and indoor swimming pool and the building surrounding it will house separate private rooms for two girls with a private bathroom, administrative offices, and class rooms."

"Oh Mary, this is so wonderful, but where will the money come from?" Sister Madelyn cried emotionally.

"Don't worry about that. The entire project is being funded and donated by a group of people who prefer to remain anonymous," Dinosa replied.

Sister Madelyn crossed herself and looking to the heaven exclaimed, "Oh Saint Mary, Mother of God, thank you for sending us such a grand benefactor."

The other Sisters crossed themselves and in unison said, "Amen."

"This," Dinosa said pointing at a skyway, "will connect the building we're in to the new one. Oh," she continued flipping through the blue prints, "let me show you the plans for the girl's rooms…"

Sol Goldsmith refilled the glasses of George Armstrong and Sean O'Farrell, topped off his own and sat back down in the easy chair of his den in his Cliff House Avenue home in San Francisco.

"Well, it's good news to hear Ian and Grant are doing well. It's just too bad we couldn't have had a heroes welcoming parade when they all got home," he remarked.

"Actually the news even gets better. That message our guys left behind in Guatemala and in Nigeria has really caught on. Reports are coming in from all over the world that vigilante groups are attacking and leaving the same note on sex slave traffickers, even from some Middle East countries," Armstrong reported.

"Maybe we can't throw them a parade, but for what it's worth, here's a toast to our team and Los Santos, Bernard Rusk," Sean said raising his glass.

Goldsmith snickered and said, "I wonder how Jamal Franks and Joey Wang would feel if they knew the Tanaka's had diverted all their off shore funds to our foundation and the money was being used to build modern facilities at centers around the country to help the very same girls they attempted to exploit."

About twenty miles south of Goldsmith's home, while changing the dressing on Ian's back and shaved head, Dinosa said, "Some of these are going to leave ugly scars."

He was lying on his stomach on a patio lounge on the deck in the back of their Pacifica beach home. Dinosa knelt beside him, gently and meticulously dressing and applying a medicinal salve on each wound. The waves were breaking rhythmically on the beach below and the sun sat glowing on the ocean's horizon. Ian lay comfortably with his folded hands cradling one side of his head as he soaked in the beautiful view, wincing only slightly when Dinosa touched a sensitive area.

"You know Mary," Ian started reflectively, "its times like this that I realize just what a lucky guy I am. I'm thinking of those poor girls who suffered so much at the hands of those radical terrorists who perpetrated such atrocities on them in the name of some crazy, fucked up religious ideology. Do you really think we are making a difference?"

Mary tilted her head in a moment of thought and replied, "For the girls we saved I believe we made a hell of a difference."

A tear trickled out of one eye and slowly drifted down her cheek and she said softly, "I believe it was old Chuck Chalmers who taught me this prayer; *Lord, give me the serenity to accept the things I cannot change, the courage to change the things I can, and the wisdom to know the difference.*"